THE BROKEN PANTHEON

BOOK ONE

ADAM BERG

CARPE VITAM
PRESS LTD

ACKNOWLEDGMENTS

Yikes.

This book started six years ago with two things—a prayer and an unchecked box on my bucket list.

I had no idea how long this little adventure would take. I only knew that I wanted to write a book and that I wanted it to bring people joy.

356 hours later (Yes, I counted), I finished my first draft. It was a mess, but I thought the bulk of my work was behind me. Sometimes I am dumb.

I wish I could remember all the help I've received over the years. I can't and I feel very guilty about this fact. Many friends read drafts and gave notes and I would like to thank all of them—in a very lame blanket statement. (Sorry!)

I will mention some people by name, because their help was more recent, and again, I have the dumbs.

Clarissa and Connie, two friends with endless insight and patience.

Mike Dalton, Dave Vance, Natalie Madsen, Tori Pence, Ava Wilstead, and Kaela Wilstead. Thank you for helping me smooth out some of the rough edges. Please never read this book again in case I failed to properly incorporate your notes. I tried.

My two editors, Sarah Reynolds and Loretta Porter. I left exactly one typo in the book just to drive both of you crazy. Try and find it.

My family, who taught me about both family and God. Much of my own experience became the spine of this story. This book grew into its own thing, but its origins can and should be traced back to my family.

Finally, let me thank my dog, Mycroft. He was no help at all, but the original title of this book was 'Mycroft's Big Adventure', so I guess he deserves a mention and some head pats.

Happy reading!

For Mike Dalton,

A true friend and the first person to ever read one of my books.

CHAPTER ONE

THE PUZZLE BOX

Hagano peered past his brother, catching glimpses of people he once considered friends. As if they could sense his stare, one by one their eyes met his and darted away on contact. The city guards hustled in and out of the cavernous room carved into The Mountain Temple. Through a buzz of excitement, they coordinated the thousand tasks required to run the capitol during the festival. Hagano's shoulders tensed. A flurry of white clothes with black accents whirled in his periphery.

"It's a puzzle box." Hagano's older brother extended a hand, a small wooden box perched on his palm. "I know I'm a few weeks late, but happy eighteenth."

The buzz of the room faded to the back of Hagano's mind. The box absorbed every ounce of attention as his thoughts instinctively went to work solving the puzzle in front of him. Intricate etching decorated the near perfect cube, but failed to hide grooves in the wood that hinted at movable pieces.

Hagano took the box and twisted it to see every surface. One, two, three—without thinking he'd assigned numbers to each supposed clue. Four, five, six—nine clues in total. A carving of the avian god, Ecret, covered the top of the box. His wings extended to the sides. His human face, adorned with five horns and half-covered by a mask, outlined what might be the first movable piece.

"Do you like it?" Hagano's brother, Alessi, chewed on his lip. His voice pulled Hagano out of his entranced stare.

"Yes." Hagano rested the box atop his injured arm, securing it inside a sling well-worn after months of use. "Thank you."

The hum of the room returned. Hagano scanned the stone corridors, the wooden tables covered in old books, the torches on the walls and the scorch marks surrounding them. The blur of movement drew his eye. Guards old and young avoided him, the one expelled from their ranks by injury.

He tugged at the strap around his neck. A jolt of pain shot through his shoulder and down his arm as if thinking about the pain brought it back to life.

"So." Alessi clasped his hands together. "You have a delivery?"

Hagano nodded and unstrapped a sword from his back. The weight of it sunk into his bones. Though light in his hand, it was nothing more than a reminder of his failure to graduate from guard training. Two years of learning combat, regulations, and policing ethics all wasted in the second it took an ornery horse to kick him in the shoulder. In what seemed like a cosmic joke, today would have been the day he received his own sword with the other trainees. Instead, he'd spent three months recovering and delivering mail, all leading to this moment—handing over someone else's sword instead of receiving his own.

"Oh?" Alessi looked over the weapon. "That's odd. All the new recruit swords were already delivered." Alessi walked over to a guard sorting papers at a desk. "Will you figure out why we have a sword delivered today?"

The guard nodded.

"So, how are things... at home?" Alessi leaned against the table.

"Good." Hagano eyed Alessi up and down, sizing him for the first time in weeks. Three year's Hagano's senior, the new lieutenant looked more ragged than rugged. Even with baggy brown eyes and greasy black hair, the girls swooned. "You know you can stop by anytime."

"I know." Alessi looked away. "It's just been busy."

Liar. Hagano clenched his jaw. He knew Alessi felt guilty about Hagano's shoulder and hadn't yet figured out how to be around him —or their parents. Lucky for Alessi, being a guard meant living in the Mountain Temple and away from his maimed brother. Hagano had only his dog to comfort him. And his parents, but they were frail and he never wanted to put extra stress on their shoulders.

The guard at the table handed Alessi a document.

Halfway down the page, Alessi's eyes squinted. "Oh." He slapped the sheet of paper back onto the desk.

"What is it?" Hagano craned his neck to try and read whatever startled Alessi.

"Nothing." Alessi's tone drifted upward.

"What is it?" Hagano reached for the paper. No one had as much experience detecting Alessi's lies.

"Let me walk you out." Alessi sprang to his feet. He placed a hand on Hagano's back and pushed him towards the exit of the guard quarters. "I'm so sorry."

"For what?" Hagano pushed his back against his brother's hand, but kept moving. "Well." Alessi cleared his throat. "It seems there was some sort of mix-up with the blacksmith. The number of new recruits we gave him was old information."

The bustling guard quarters gave way to a giant, hollow chamber, home to Lord Ecret's hanging stalactite throne.

"What do you mean?" Hagano came to a full stop. His voice echoed through the chamber.

Alessi's eyes wandered until settling their gaze on the floor. "There was..." He licked his lips. "There was one less recruit than expected."

It was Hagano. His heart sank. He was the missing recruit and the sword was supposed to be his. His faced flushed—suddenly warm. "Ah."

"I'm so sorry, Hagano." Alessi's voice trembled. "If I... you shouldn't... maybe you could reenlist once you recover –"

"Don't." Hagano put up his good hand. "Please." He hadn't yet told Alessi the entirety of the healer's prognosis. His shoulder would perpetually weaken. He'd never again meet the physical requirements to become a guard.

"But you were so close to graduating."

Hagano stared down his brother.

A warm voice filled the room. "Protocol suggests that you keep it." Ecret flew overhead, soaring out of a dark corner of the ceiling and over to the brothers. He landed next to them, standing at twice their height. He had the face of a man, but the body of a giant crane. Luminous white feathers blended into a cowl that covered his head. Five black horns cut through the cowl, forming a jagged crown. A glimmering orange glow illuminated his eyes, just above the mask that covered his nose and descended his elongated neck. The tips of his wings glistened black.

Hagano and Alessi bowed. Every time Hagano came face to face with Ecret felt like coming home to a warm hearth on a cold day. The god radiated serenity. His glow hushed the noise of the world—and the noise in Hagano's heart.

Ecret reached a talon into the air toward the hall that led to the guard station. A sword flew from the hall and into Ecret's grip.

Confused, Hagano looked up at the sword in Ecret's talon. "Lord?"

Ecret extended it to Hagano. "Stand."

Rising, Hagano reached for the sword but pulled back his hand. "I'm a courier, not a guard." He motioned to his shoulder. "I can't."

The god lowered his head, looking Hagano squarely in the eyes. "Did you know that retired guards keep their swords?"

Hagano shook his head. "No. I didn't."

"Some are injured in their service and forced to retire. But the sword is theirs for life." Ecret turned to Alessi. "Would you mind excusing us for a moment, lieutenant?"

"Yes, Lord." Alessi rose, bowed his head, and vanished into the guard hall.

Hagano forced a smile, still uncertain about what the sword meant. "Thank you."

"Do you mind if I ask how you were injured?" Ecret's voice filled Hagano's chest with a lightness that nearly buoyed him in the air. It sounded like two melodious voices speaking in unison.

"I was in training." The memory dredged up sorrow, undoing the comfort in Ecret's voice. "I was working at the stables. Lieutenant Alessi, my brother, had given me the assignment to work with a particularly difficult horse. The horse bucked me off. And as I stood back up, it kicked me... in my shoulder."

Ecret nodded. "You're lucky."

Lucky? Had it not been Ecret who said it, Hagano would have rolled his eyes. He knew what came next. It was always the same—be thankful that he wasn't kicked in the head or the chest or in some worse manner. It wasn't an argument Hagano could fight, but a life-altering injury was far from lucky.

Ecret squinted, forming happy wrinkles around his eyes. "Most people struggle to remember the most important thing in life."

Hagano's brows furrowed.

"Every time your shoulder hurts, let it remind you of the eternal bliss that awaits once you die and I carry you to paradise. There will be no pain, Hagano, not for the pious."

Something dormant stirred inside Hagano, erasing a layer of grief. "Thank you. I only hope to live well enough to deserve such a reward."

"I hope so too."

It was hard to tell beneath the mask, but Hagano could have sworn the god was smiling.

"And don't hold it against your brother. It wasn't his fault, even though he thinks it is." Ecret stretched out his massive wings. "Brothers can be difficult, but remember to be grateful. You might not always have the luxury of having him around."

Hagano nodded. He wasn't sure what to say. If he were honest with himself, he did blame Alessi for the accident. He also missed his brother immensely now that they didn't both live at home.

"Is that a puzzle box sitting in your sling?" The tip of Ecret's wing pointed at Hagano's resting arm.

Hagano looked down at the box, almost forgetting it was there.

"May I?" The puzzle box lifted itself.

Hagano nodded.

The box floated into the air, disappearing behind a swirl of feathers. It reappeared at Ecret's eye level, spinning, and twisting as if Ecret's mind also got lost in an attempt to solve it.

"Hmm." Ecret exhaled. "You must be fond of puzzles."

A chill ran up Hagano's spine as if the god had performed an unexplainable magic trick. "I am." He cleared his throat. "How did you know?"

The puzzle box drifted back to Hagano's sling. He half-expected the god to have solved the puzzle, but its pieces remained locked.

Ecret crouched, looking Hagano in the eyes. "Everything is a puzzle, young Hagano. A box. A conversation. Some might even say the world. The question is, can you see the clues?"

"Clues to what?" The box floated back into Hagano's sling.

The god stood upright. "All clues point to the same thing—the truth."

Words failed to form on Hagano's tongue. He wanted to ask what the god meant, but couldn't seem to phrase the question.

"It is time for me to go." Ecret looked past Hagano. "And you'd best join the other guards for the commencement."

A warmth returned to Hagano's chest. He'd long dreamed of sitting with the guards during the annual festival. Though not destined to serve the city, he now had his sword and a spot among his peers.

"Every piece has its place." The nail of Ecret's talon tapped the box. "Best go take yours."

CHAPTER TWO

THE DAY OF DELIVERANCE

The chill of the cavernous throne room dissipated as Hagano stepped outside and into the sunlight. To his left, the steeple of the temple, The Sky Spear, towered over the whole city. A wide staircase descended in front of him, spilling onto a flat plaza. At its center stood a statue of Lord Ecret, wings outstretched, standing atop a defeated, cloaked figure—The Sylph King.

A sea of people buzzed as bodies filled the city streets. Upbeat music danced in the air, punctuating the drone of a thousand conversations.

Hagano shielded his eyes from the noon sun as he eyed the plaza. On the stairs to his left sat a congregation of clergymen, dressed in the traditional garb of the festival as well as their usual headdress. To his right sat a myriad of guards, new boots and seasoned veterans, side-by-side. With each step, Hagano searched for a group that looked welcoming. One by one, they avoided his gaze or flashed an uncomfortable smile as if to tell him to look elsewhere. At the far end of the guard area, an empty section called his name.

He gripped his new sword and sat down by himself. The puzzle box nearly fell out of his sling, but he caught it with his free hand. Bringing it to where his injured hand could touch it, he played with it. Rubbing his thumbs over each surface, only one piece budged—the part of the box depicting Ecret's body. He slid the piece out of its home and tucked it away in his sling. With the first part gone, other pieces found new room to move.

"Now there's a face I'm not familiar with." The cheery voice of a woman pulled Hagano's attention. "And here I thought I knew all of the graduates." She sat next to him and extended a hand. "I'm Jaga."

"Hagano." He shook her hand, trying to remember her face. In all his time in training, he didn't remember meeting her. Her dark skin, short hair, and forty-something-year-old demeanor did nothing to help. A wooden staff at her back drew his eye. He'd assumed she was a guard, but they all carried swords. Maybe she wasn't one. "Oh." Her comment about being a graduate caught up to him. "I'm not a guard." His eyes darted to his bad shoulder and back to her.

Jaga sat back. "Neither am I. At least not anymore. Though I do try to keep up on things." Her calm tone and relaxed posture showed no sign of discomfort.

Hagano was far too accustomed to people tensing up over the faux pas of drawing attention to his injury. A flash of regret always lit in their eyes the moment they realized his story was something of a tragedy. But not Jaga. She seemed unfazed. Perhaps it was the fact she was about twice Hagano's age. Or perhaps she was accustomed to having unpleasant conversations. Then again, maybe she had mastered her bluffing face and knew how to hide what was really going on inside. In any case, Hagano found himself at ease. "So you used to be a guard?"

"Yep." Jaga crossed her legs. "Retired a few years ago—younger than most, I know, but it was time."

"Mmhm." Hagano slid the removed puzzle piece back into the box and rested it on his arm. "So, where's your sword?" He pointed his chin at the staff.

Reaching back, Jaga pointed at her weapon with a thumb. "I don't much like fighting with a sword. Much prefer a wooden weapon."

"Really?" Hagano had to consciously keep himself from sounding condescending. "Doesn't that put you at a disadvantage?"

She shook her head slowly—again unfazed by Hagano's question. If she were as familiar with the new guards as she said, she must be used to this question. "A weapon is only as good as the wielder."

"Ah." Her comment rang true, even if it didn't clear up his confusion as to why she'd prefer a wooden staff over a metal sword. "That makes sense."

The booming of drums burst through the air. At the opposite end of the plaza, a line of drummers beat their mallets against a line of snake-skinned drums. The music echoed through the plaza and off the mountains.

Jaga leaned closer to Hagano. "Sounds like it's starting."

"Yeah." He exhaled. "It was nice to meet you." He extended his hand.

She glanced at it. "If it's all the same to you, I'd like to stay here for The Commencement."

"Oh." Hagano whipped back his hand. "Of course." It felt like someone was squeezing the innards in his chest. He assumed she'd be off to sit with friends or family, but here she stayed and now it looked like Hagano was trying to get rid of her. "I didn't mean to," he whispered.

"Shhh." She winked and pointed at the temple gates above, focusing on the festival.

The musicians played a song familiar to anyone who had attended a service presided over by one of Ecret's hierophants. Their song declared them as leaders of all things spiritual and governmental. Hierophants came and went as old age caught up to them, but Ecret always had five and they were always selected from the most devoted of his disciples.

Through the gates appeared four old men dressed in both the festival garb and the tokens of their positions. The first was the Crown, the Head of the Hierophant Council. An onyx halo adorned his head. Five wooden branches grew out of its base. This particular man had served on the council the longest and it showed in his fattened belly and wobbling steps.

At the Crown's left walked Ecret's speaker, the Maxilla. Any of

Ecret's decrees would be written by his hand, which is why the right sleeve of his garment had been replaced by a web of gold and silver strings coiling down his arm.

Behind them walked the Auricle and the Rachis. The first served as Ecret's ears, listening to and fulfilling the needs of the people. An empty vial hung from his neck, a symbolic vessel that would catch the people's prayers and also pour out Lord Ecret's blessings. The Rachis carried two books, one full of history and the other left blank for the history not yet written.

As a child, Hagano dreamed of serving as The Rachis—the one charged with keeping records. His affinity for the temple library made him a natural fit, but aspiring for something as lofty as a member of Ecret's council felt out of reach. The memory of this wish sat uncomfortably next to his failure as a guard. He chewed on his lip.

The four hierophants waved at the people in all directions as they sauntered over to the five thrones sitting at the front of the gathering.

The empty seat stood out to Hagano in a way that tugged at the corners of his mind. A wave of stupor struck him as he tried to reason why one of the hierophants was missing. In all his eighteen years of attending the festival, he couldn't recall ever seeing one absent. The Hallux, the head of law enforcement, was not present. The only explanation that his brain could muster was that the old man must have fallen ill.

Trumpets sounded. Drums thundered to a new beat. The people roared in anticipation.

Out of the dark temple chambers walked Lord Ecret, the avian-god of the people of Ecretia. His radiance shone bright, even against the light of the beating sun. He walked gracefully, his wings floating weightlessly at his side.

Ecret's appearance brought a silence with it. The entire population submitted to his tranquil presence. The god bowed before his people. Then, without a word, he unfolded his wings and jumped into the sky.

Every eye fixated on his every move. Ecret swam through the air to every corner of the city, allowing all to see him on this celebratory day.

Regardless of how far their god flew, the people remained quiet.

Ecret circled back. With unwavering elegance, he landed at the temple grounds, taking his place in front of the hierophants.

My friends. Ecret's voice entered Hagano's thoughts, filling him with its familiar, calming warmth. *How wonderful it is to see you here on this day.*

In the blink of an eye, a falling body appeared in the sky at Ecret's back.

A horrid thud cracked across the courtyard as the body crashed into the temple steps. An elderly man, a hierophant, lay bleeding mere yards away from Hagano's seat. The man's neck had broken. His skull lay open. He wheezed his last breath as the life in his aged eyes retreated inward.

A wave of fear paralyzed every bone in Hagano's body. Was this real? Was he asleep at home—his mind conjuring a nightmare? His stomach twisted. A weight sunk into his lungs. He'd stopped breathing. He gasped for air as his eyes looked to the four men in the five thrones, assuming that the dying hierophant was the missing one. No. There were only three men. And a woman, a young woman with markings on her face – someone he didn't recognize, sitting in the Rachis' seat. And the Rachis was now dying on the temple steps, having inexplicably fallen out of the sky.

Hagano's heart sank into his gut. It made no sense. He could hardly form a thought before people started screaming. He looked in the one direction he could for answers—toward his god. As his eyes found Ecret, Hagano caught sight of the remaining hierophants clawing at their throats. A sizzling black tar ate into each of their necks, sending them into a blind panic as they vainly fought for life.

Smiling, the woman next to them nestled into her seat.

CHAPTER THREE
AN UNCEREMONIOUS RETURN

Thin streams of black tar slithered out of the hierophants' throats and wrapped around the woman's hands. Her festival garb made her blend in with the horrified onlookers, but tattoos on her face proved how much she didn't belong. Dark lines inked paths from her inner eyelids to the corners of her mouth. Two lines dripped down her cheeks from the outside of her eyes and two dots marked the space between her brows—mimicking the patterns of a cheetah.

The tar entered her mouth and disappeared down her throat. She stood with the poise of a seasoned combatant. The bodies of the old men smoked at her feet. An eerie hush fell over the crowd as people stared with gaping mouths.

A downpour of thoughts flooded Hagano's mind. Six hundred years of peace gone in an instant—during his lifetime—an idea so strange he'd never entertained it before. But who could this woman be? The Sylph King was long defeated. Who else was there?

Ecret whipped his head toward his dead servants. He circled in front of the woman and thrust a talon, but the cheetah-faced woman vanished. In her place stood a toddler, no older than two, looking confused as a rush of emotion flushed his cheeks and forced cries from his mouth.

Ecret pulled back, keeping the child from harm. His eyes searched the crowd for the now missing woman.

An ounce of clarity found its way to Hagano, releasing him from his fearful paralysis. He looked to Jaga, thinking she might know if he should run or sit still, panic or trust that his god would protect him. She dashed away, disappearing into the crowd without a word.

The sounds of retching pulled Hagano's attention to the plaza center. The cheetah-faced woman sat atop the statue of Ecret defeating The Sylph King. Hunched over, she spewed black tar onto the ground. Spinning around, she created a circle of bubbling blackness on the ground. The dirt below her smoked and sizzled, melting through everything it touched. As the smoke rose, a gray veil masked her, creating the silhouette of a woman that thinned and slumped as if she too were melting.

A thunderous crack cut through the air. The ground rumbled.

"Stand back." Ecret's voice permeated the crowd. It wrapped around Hagano like a blanket, calming his racing heart.

The smoke thinned into wisps. The woman was gone. And so was the statue. In its place was nothing more than a gaping pit and the unearthly howl of wind bellowing from its depths.

A clang echoed up from the chasm.

Ecret fluttered to the hole and stared silently into it. Everyone else backed away, their attention split between their savior and the sounds of the pit.

Another clang rang out. The shrill sounds of metal scraping metal screeched and echoed.

Then silence.

Dark clouds gathered, blotting out the sun and leaving the world in a gloom.

A shadow shot out of the pit and landed opposite Ecret. The figure hunched over, cloaked in darkness. Old bones hung from its neck, clung to its arms, and protruded from its head. Dozens of rusted swords stabbed into its back. There was no mistake — this was The Sylph King.

Everyone rushed to escape. Some cried for loved ones. Others cried for Ecret. The chaos knocked some to the ground, leaving them to be trampled.

Hagano tried to move, but couldn't. He kept telling his legs to run but anxiety held him hostage. He wanted to flee or hide or help, but his body and mind wouldn't connect. Something, somewhere inside him told him to fight. A nagging thought popped into his head, reminding him that he knew how to use a sword and after years of effort, he finally had his own. But he couldn't, not with his bad arm.

"We don't need to retread this path." Ecret spread his wings as if to take flight.

"Yes, we do." The Sylph King stomped a foot underneath its shadowy robes.

Another rumbling shook the earth until a stone platform rose out of the pit. Dozens of soldiers stood atop it. No, not soldiers, sylphs— the king's servants. They looked like people, but were no longer human. Dead souls, kept from paradise and warped by death into mindless slaves.

The Sylph King launched himself at Ecret. He grabbed the god's neck, flinging both of them into the air. They smacked against the temple walls, sending a cascade of stones down onto the people below.

The guards drew their weapons, prompting Hagano to do the same.

His racing heart sent waves of blood pounding through his bad shoulder. The thumping woke the pain, making it throb with every heartbeat. He wrapped his injured arm around his ribs, wishing he could brace it more comfortably.

You can fight. You can fight. You can fight. The mantra took over his thoughts as his sword shook in his trembling grip.

The guards near the sylph battalion arranged themselves into formation. Captains shouted, commanding groups to prepare for a fight.

The world blurred.

"Hagano." Alessi's voice called out from the chaos.

Dumbstruck, Hagano turned to his brother.

"You need to go." Alessi tugged Hagano's arm and pointed to a path on the far end of the plaza that would lead home.

"Go?" The word lost all meaning. His mind blanked. "G-go where?" Hagano renewed the grip on his sword.

"Home, Hagano. Take care of mom and dad. I'll be there as soon —"

"Lieutenant." Another voice shouted, capturing Alessi's attention.

"I have to go." Alessi nudged Hagano before rushing back into the madness.

You can fight. He looked down the path Alessi had pointed to. Citizens flocked to its safety. *You can fight.* He looked back to the guards just as sylphs and swords began to clash.

A shattering quake rattled the ground beneath Hagano's feet. At the temple steps, Ecret and The Sylph King wrestled. They traded blows with such force that the world quivered from each impact.

Attacking Ecret made no sense. Gods can't die. They're immortal. There was only one possible outcome to this fight and that was Ecret defeating The Sylph King a second time.

Hagano looked out to the crowd and the pandemonium around him. *You can fight.* The face of a man caught his eye—a still face, a calm face. The man's vacant expression chilled Hagano's spine. It was not the expression of a man.

The sylph vaulted into the guards' area. A battalion of sylphs flanked him.

Hagano swallowed hard. Without thinking, he stepped away.

"Stand your ground, coward!" One of the guards shouted his way.

You can fight.

The guards and the sylphs clashed haphazardly. Despite not carrying weapons, the sylphs fended off their attackers without the slightest sign of effort. One kicked a guard to the ground and stomped her heel into the fallen soldier's head. Another guard sliced off one sylph's arm only to be spattered by black blood that dissolved the guard's clothes and skin.

You... can fight. The power of the words faltered.

An unoccupied sylph locked its gaze on Hagano. The sylph

pushed both guards and cohorts aside as it stared at Hagano and made his way to him. A puzzled look crossed the sylph's face, making Hagano wilt.

You...

Hagano scrambled to hold out his sword. The sweat in his palm kept it from staying still. A fight for his life stood but a few feet away. The drumming of his heart beat in his ears and thumped against his pained shoulder. His breath shortened.

Doubts threatened to defeat him before the sylph even lifted a finger. He wasn't skilled enough to kill an enemy. Even if he were, his injury could prove fatally hindering. As far as he could tell, none of the soldiers put up much of a fight and they had finished training.

Ecret willing, you can do this. Hagano planted his feet and stood in a defensive position. A jolt of energy shot through him. Was it adrenaline? Conviction? Confidence? Whatever it was, his hands steadied.

"Hagano," Alessi shouted, drawing the attention of the sylph.

The creature turned to face Alessi.

Now's your chance. Hagano charged the sylph, sword first.

The lifeless man whipped back to Hagano, grabbing the blade, and stopped it mid strike. The sylph peered into Hagano's eyes with a hollow stare. He clenched the blade, letting it cut through his skin. The wound seeped tar, corroding the steel.

Another blade shot out of the sylph's chest and up toward Hagano's face. He fell backward as Alessi cut through the sylph's torso. Despite the wound, the sylph clamored to attack. His arms and head twitched before falling still on the ground.

Alessi held up his melted sword. "Are you okay?"

Hagano nodded.

The stub of Alessi's sword fell from his grip and clanged on the ground. "Give me your weapon." Alessi took the blade out of Hagano's hand without waiting for permission. "And go home, Hagano. You'll be safe there."

"But..."

"I will meet you at home." Alessi stared at Hagano expectantly.

"Go through the temple and leave out of one of the side tunnels. There's no time to argue. Just go." He sprinted back into the fray.

The wave of conviction passed, giving way to a sense of dread. Hagano swallowed hard and headed towards the temple door. He pressed himself up against a stone wall, trying to avoid the action, but still found himself having to sprint past sections of the fight. Just as he neared the stairs to the main gate, the fighting crowded at the steps with no room to get through. Ducking into a secluded section of the wall, Hagano tried to reach up to the next level.

His fingers clenched onto the ledge. The wall was too tall for him to pull himself up, especially with only one arm. The stones did not protrude out in the slightest, offering no foothold. His only thought was to hop up as high as he could and hope he'd manage enough of a boost to lift himself to the top. Mustering the will to jump, something crashed into him, knocking Hagano's face into the stones and pinning him to the wall.

Everything turned black. Whatever hit Hagano pressed against him so intensely he could barely breathe, let alone move. It was warm. It was... a body, writhing and fighting for life. He couldn't see it. He couldn't tell if it was friend or foe. The sounds of weak gurgling crept into his ears. The strained wheezes of the poor soul faded until the body went limp, freeing Hagano.

He whipped around. A pale hand gripped a dead guard's neck and dropped the body to the ground. The sylph flexed his hand and cocked his head.

Hagano's eyes darted to the ledge above, then back to the sylph. He gritted his teeth. How dumb had Alessi been to take his sword? His brother had doomed him while also trying to keep him safe. If only either of them had anticipated this moment. His brother must have thought the sword useless in Hagano's hands. Shaking his head, Hagano dispelled the thought. *You can fight.*

Time slowed as Hagano and the sylph waited for each other to make a move. The sylph's eyes drifted down to the empty sheath sitting on Hagano's hip, then over to the sling holding his bad arm. Pausing for a second, the sylph kicked Hagano in the chest.

He crashed into the bricks and slid down the wall, gasping for air.

The sylph ran off towards a group of guards.

Coughing, Hagano pushed against the wall until back on his feet. Confused why the sylph spared him, he looked down at his empty sheath. Perhaps Alessi's hasty act of theft saved Hagano's life after all. Had he been armed, the sylph might have thought to kill him. That is —if sylphs even think at all.

Hagano looked down at the body of the choked guard and stepped on his back for a boost. "Sorry," he whispered as he jumped off the corpse and grabbed the ledge above. "And thank you." Hagano lifted himself up, using both hands and fighting the sharp pains in his shoulder. The strain felt like daggers up and down his arm, but he reached the top.

He jogged for the temple doors. It's interior flashed in his mind. A path from the throne room to the library lit up in his vision as clear as the world in front of him. If he could get there, he would be safe from the battle. Then he could figure out his way through one of the many side tunnels and loop back around to his house, hopefully circumventing the battle completely.

The first chamber came into view as Hagano neared the entrance. The familiar scene of Ecret's hanging throne and the many statues of hierophants welcomed him. Windows and fires illuminated the room, paying special attention to the holy figures carved inside. The artistry was unparalleled, the décor more ornate than any object made by man. The beauty of the room soothed Hagano as he fled the horrors at his back.

The moment he stepped foot in the temple, The Sylph King crashed through the ceiling into the center of the room, cutting off Hagano's escape. Rubble fell from the new hole in the building, landing atop the shadowy demon.

Hagano turned back, running at full speed away from the hideous monstrosity. Guards and sylphs clashed on the temple steps. Ecret circled in the sky above. There was nowhere to turn.

His shoulder throbbed.

The Sylph King reappeared on the top of the temple, standing in the hole his body just created. "Show me the endling!"

A deafening burst erupted from the side of the temple. The stonework shifted and collected itself, assembling into thousands of small figures shaped like mixtures of spiders and scorpions. The stone creatures swarmed, spreading out and flinging themselves at sylphs.

Ecret landed swiftly at the entrance of the temple. His arrival sent a wave of dust and wind in all directions.

The trunk of a tree cracked through the ground at the plaza center below, growing into a tower in seconds. Dozens of branches shot out from its base, snapping and creaking as they burst into existence. They slithered through the air with the speed of vipers, making their way towards each and every sylph.

At long last, Lord Ecret's power was in full force.

Hope ignited inside Hagano. *Ecret will fix this. He'll fix everything.*

A handful of sylphs charged at the god, dodging the tree branches that chased them.

The stone spiders interceded, launching themselves onto the sylphs and piercing their bodies with a flurry of jagged pincers.

Even in battle, Ecret's majesty never wavered. He was powerful, holy, unstoppable. No one had seen him fight for centuries. Not since the sealing of The Sylph King. It was nothing short of a marvel, watching a god use his powers. Now Hagano was witness to Ecret's godhood.

The Sylph King dropped from the sky and landed on Ecret. A deafening burst rattled the air, as the collision sent the pair deep into the earth and out of sight.

An eerie moment of quiet passed.

Hagano looked toward the spot where Ecret and The Sylph King disappeared.

The avian god reemerged from the hole, battered and bleeding. He gawkily stepped forward before leaping into the air. He flew in arcs, reaching up to the sky, then dipping down to the ground to drag his talon in the dirt and flutter his wings over his frightened people. The god rose and fell, swooping closer and closer to Hagano.

The sight of the approaching god warmed Hagano's chest. With one claw, the god scraped the ground. With the other, Ecret reached for Hagano and clasped onto his face, dragging him across the dirt. A surge of panic swelled. He couldn't see anything. He could only feel the rush of wind, the hard dirt grazing his feet, and the leathery grip of the avian god. A pang of fear pierced him, not knowing what was happening and wondering if he would survive.

A blast of energy shot out of Ecret's talon and into Hagano's body.

The taste of burnt flesh coated his tongue. A burning heat accompanied it.

"Eat," echoed a melodic voice from the depths of Hagano's mind —a voice he had never heard.

The searing pain spread from his tongue, down his throat and into his stomach.

"Eat," commanded the voice again.

The line between the world and Hagano thinned. The energies of each part of the plaza converged on him as if they were part of his own body. The earth gave him a taste of antiquity. Ecret emanated unfathomable power. The people felt like an incarnation of innocence. The sky offered a touch of infinity. The Sylph King felt like a beacon of anger. A myriad of textures washed over his skin—soft and prickly, coarse and smooth.

"Eat," said the voice again, as if from a distance.

Everything disappeared from Hagano's view until only darkness remained. Out of the darkness stretched the back of a glowing, clenched fist. The luminous hand bore no blemish.

The hand turned over and extended its fingers, revealing the body of a small fish.

"Eat." Repeated the voice, without echo or faintness.

The vision of the hand vanished. The darkness faded. Hagano's connection to the world severed.

He awoke in the rubble at the temple entrance. The bizarreness of his experience dizzied his head. His muscles ached. His stomach churned, but burned no longer. He squinted, bringing the world into focus.

Piles of stone spiders decorated the battlefield. Hundreds of bodies filled the courtyard, the plaza, and the streets. Nearby homes and buildings had collapsed, some leaving not two bricks together. Pained moans and mournful wails lingered in the air. The Sylph King stood on the temple steps. Ecret's body lay motionless at his feet.

Hagano's body wouldn't move. He couldn't stand. His shoulder threatened to explode. He craned his neck to look at The Sylph King. A pit in his stomach weighed heavy on his shivering frame. This was a nightmare. It had to be. He clenched his jaw, fighting back tears.

That demonic shadow lifted Ecret's limp body with one hand. He turned his neck to face the temple and flung the dead god into the walls as if Ecret was nothing more than a pebble.

The god's corpse broke more temple stones and flopped onto the ground. Then nothing. No movement. No recovery. No life at all.

No. Hagano hugged himself—his arms trembling. *Ecret? Lord?*

The Sylph King walked slowly up the temple steps, past Hagano, over Ecret's corpse, and into the temple. The cheetah-faced woman followed with sylphs in their wake.

Hagano's mind blanked. Under any other circumstance he would pray. Now he could do nothing but look at the dead, feathered, bloodied creature in the dirt.

CHAPTER FOUR
DEATH OF THE PSYCHOPOMP

Blood drained from Hagano's head, leaving a daze behind. He fought back tears as he looked out to Ecret's lifeless, bloodied corpse, finding it impossible not to stare. One wing slumped over the god's chest, contorted in a way that no living creature would find comfortable. The other wing sprawled out over the temple steps with missing feathers.

The strange vision of the hand and the fish prevented Hagano from seeing his god's demise, but the scene before him filled in the gaps. The Sylph King won—somehow. Hagano swallowed. His gut churned. Ecret wasn't immortal... anymore? Or had he never been? No. A faint warmth in his chest brought Hagano's faith to the forefront. If Ecret had never been immortal, then he preached lies. That wasn't Ecret. It only made sense that whatever power made Ecret immortal had failed or had been stolen. Hagano shook his head. His mind felt fuzzy. None of this made sense.

His breath quickened as panic surged. *Alessi.* His brother's name funneled every frantic thought into one purpose—he needed to find Alessi. Sitting up, the aches in his shoulder turned into sharp pains. He winced.

Faint cries echoed from every direction. Dead bodies littered the steps, the plaza, everywhere. A gathering stood at Ecret's side, weeping on bent knees.

An injured guard limped closer to Hagano, panting. Burnt skin marred his face as if someone had splattered acid on him.

Hagano cleared his throat. He couldn't think of how to help the frail guard—or anyone. His thoughts couldn't shake his worry for his brother. "Have you seen Lieutenant Alessi?" Hagano's knees trembled as he forced himself to his feet. The puzzle box, still nestled in his sling, started to slip out. He pushed it back. "He looks like me, but taller. Same brown skin. Black, greasy hair. He's a guard like you. Like--" he wanted to say 'us', but the word didn't come out.

The guard's sunken eyes drifted to the ground as he shrugged.

Hagano tensed. He let out a jittering breath. Alessi was missing, maybe gone—forever. Was he dead? Was his body draped over a piece of rubble? Was he disfigured like the man in front of him, too warped to recognize? He bit his lip.

No. That was bad thinking. One guard didn't know Alessi's whereabouts. It meant nothing. Alessi could be alive and well for all he knew.

Holding his head, Hagano forced himself to walk over to a woman lying on the ground bracing her mangled leg. "Have you seen Lieutenant Alessi?"

She scrunched her face. It flushed red. "Help me. Can you...?" She groaned. "I need help."

The plea choked Hagano. He didn't know what to do, nor whom to look for. "I..." No words came. "I..."

Another guard approached. She leaned down to her injured comrade, then looked back up to Hagano. "I will take care of her." She snapped her fingers at Hagano, making him blink. "You go home."

Nodding, Hagano backed away slowly.

Go home, Hagano. Alessi's voice echoed in his mind.

Home. His parents. They could help. They... didn't know what had happened. They stopped attending the festival last year so they didn't have to fight the crowds in their old age. For once their feeble-ness was a blessing.

A chorus of wails rang out from where Ecret laid. The group at his side lifted daggers into the air, plunged them into their stomachs, and toppled over.

Hagano squeezed his eyes shut. Why would they do that? Why add to the suffering? Why doom their spirits when Ecret was gone and could no longer ferry them to paradise?

He needed to leave, catch his breath, clear his mind, and find his brother. His feet ached. His vision blurred. *Return home.* That was the only thought he'd allow himself to think. He wiped his face, smearing his fingers with the orange paint put there for the celebration.

The farther he walked along the main road, the quicker his pace became. By the time he reached his house, enough strength found him to burst into a jog. The wooden door to his humble family home called out to him. The ounce of familiarity was enough to sooth his nerves.

Throwing open the door, he yelled, "Alessi?!"

His father jolted in his chair at the kitchen table, dropped his knife and clutched his chest. The bubbling of a stew at the hearth reached Hagano's ears.

"Is Alessi here?" Hagano looked down the hallway hoping his brother would step out of one of the bedrooms.

"He was just here, looking for you." Hagano's father took his cane and limped over to him.

"Is he alright? Is he hurt? I couldn't find him." The words spilled out of Hagano's mouth, blending together into near babbling. But Alessi was alive. That fact alone let Hagano breathe.

His father nodded. "He's alright. Roughed up, but fine. He was more concerned about you."

"I have to go find him." Hagano looked to the door, not sure where to start his search.

His father placed a calming hand on Hagano's back. "No, Hagano, sit down."

"I can't."

"Alessi told me to keep you here. He'll be back as soon as he can." His father guided Hagano to a chair by the kitchen table.

He sat, but his legs struggled to stay still.

"What's going on, Hagano?" His dad settled back into his seat. "Alessi looked so worried about you, but he was in and out of here before he could stop and explain."

Words could barely form in Hagano's head, let alone his mouth. He played with his jaw. "Something's happened." Sweat beaded at his neck.

"I gathered that much." His dad nodded, putting on the same face he did when Hagano was a child and would come to him with a scraped knee.

"Whatever it is…" His mother's voice came from the hallway. She stepped into the kitchen and put a hand on the back of her husband's chair. "Lord Ecret will take care of it." Her eyes met Hagano's face and shifted from pacifying to concerned. "Hagano, look at you." She gathered a rag from a drawer, dipped it in a wash basin and went to work cleaning Hagano's brow.

The muscles in his face went slack, wiping away all expression. He stared down at the table—at diced vegetables and a dead chicken still in need of plucking. "He's dead."

"Alessi?" His mother shook her head. "No, he was just here."

"No." Hagano took his mother's hand. "Ecret."

Silence.

She squinted and shook her head. "Nonsense. You know just as well as I that he can't—"

"He died." The words left Hagano's mouth louder and sharper than intended.

His father's chair squeaked as he leaned back. His mother dropped her hands and retreated one step closer to her bedroom.

"He died. He was killed." Hagano shot up from his chair. The puzzle box popped out of his sling and landed on the table. "The Sylph King killed him."

"That can't be right." A light behind his mother's eyes dimmed. "You're not making sense."

"I saw it." Hagano licked the front of his teeth. "Alessi saw it. Ecret's body is just lying there... on the steps of the temple...." A stream of tears blurred his vision. "Go see for yourself if you don't believe me." Clearing his throat, he wiped his eyes.

His parents exchanged worried looks. Hagano wasn't sure his words had registered with them, even if they did not argue. His mother stepped to him, gently pulled his forehead to her lips and gave him a soft kiss. "I am going to go pray." She turned to leave.

Hagano balled his good hand into a fist. "Why?"

"Hagano." His father's tone sharpened. After a deep breath, he relaxed and returned to his normal, sweet self. "I'll be right back."

His parents entered their room and closed the door.

Dropping to his seat, Hagano rested his head on the table. His family was in trouble. They needed to run or hide or find some way to protect themselves from The Sylph King's tyranny. Ideas of fleeing the city flitted around in his head. But there was nowhere to go.

The stillness of the room wakened the pains in his body, but he had no energy left to try and ease them.

The Sylph King won. He had escaped the horrors of his own world and killed the only being standing between Hagano and paradise. Only one fate awaited Ecret's people—damnation and eternal misery. Out of their last breaths, more sylphs would be born, making The Sylph King's army that much stronger. Hagano's soul would be thrown onto a heap of spirits The Sylph King liked to torture. In time, more and more would die and he would forever be lost inside a mountain of dead bodies, unable to move or act or hope.

Fighting wasn't a thought worth considering. Ecret lost and no amount of manpower could measure up to a god. They could either sit still or run. He would need to lead his family across the Barrier Mountains, which was an impossible task on its own. *Perhaps, though, the other gods will know of Ecret's death and open the barrier to refugees. One of them could save us. Any one of them could. And there were four other gods. One was bound to show mercy.*

Hagano's old dog sauntered into the room, nearly tripping over nothing. The old mutt strutted up to Hagano, placed a paw on his leg, and sniffed the air around him.

Hagano leaned down and patted the dog on his head.

Wagging his tail, the dog walked to the corner of the table and sniffed at the dead chicken sitting atop it.

The bird, an old hen named Milena, lay flopped over. An image of a bleeding Ecret sprawled out flashed in Hagano's mind. He forced it out.

The jittering of his legs intensified. He needed something to do. The bubbling stew on the hearth caught his eye. The bird needed stripping.

"Eat," echoed a voice, the same one he heard in his mind when Ecret took him.

Hagano shook his head.

His mother's cries seeped through the wall.

He rubbed his temples and groaned. His parents were probably hungry. And Alessi would need something when he returned. *Yes. Be helpful. Keep busy. Don't think.*

Hagano walked over to the pot hanging in the hearth. Various vegetables had already been diced and placed inside. His father must have been finishing up when Hagano arrived. The only thing left was to prepare the chicken. Hagano lifted the pot out of the hearth and replaced it with one filled with water.

He dipped in his finger, testing its warmth. Still cool. He snatched the puzzle box off the table and fiddled with it while the water heated. The piece of the box designed to look like Ecret's body slipped out of place with one move of his thumb.

Everything is a puzzle, young Hagano. Ecret's words intruded on his thoughts. *A box. A conversation. Some might even say the world. The question is, can you see the clues?*

He looked down at the wooden face of Ecret. Click—one thought connected to another. A strange feeling gave him chills. Odd, it felt, to have removed Ecret from the box when Ecret had just been removed from the world. He groaned, annoyed by his own desperate thinking that everything happened for a reason. The connection between the box and Ecret's death couldn't have been anything more than coincidence. Alessi gave Hagano the box. It wasn't a divine message about Ecret's departure.

Hagano closed his eyes and pictured his last conversation with his god. *It's time for me to go.* Now the god's goodbye felt haunting—almost prophetic.

Twisting and tugging at the shifting box, not a single piece budged loose.

The water boiled. Hagano tucked the box in his sling, draped Milena across his arm, and took the pot to the small enclosure one would only generously call a backyard.

More chickens scuttled around, avoiding him. For one reason or another, fate had spared them today. At least Hagano wouldn't have to slit one of their throats and watch it flap wildly until death took it. A raccoon had done the killing for him during the night, but somehow escaped without its prize.

After retrieving a knife from the kitchen, Hagano held it to Milena's throat. A practiced prayer spilled out without thought. "Thank you for your sacrifice. Because of your death, me and my own may live." He cut into the chicken's neck and held it upside down. Blood oozed out.

Flashes of the hierophants clawing at their sizzling throats cut into his mind. He blinked rapidly, sending them away, wishing he could forget the horrid sight.

He tied the legs together with a string and hung Milena upside down on a nail sticking out of the house's back wall. The time waiting for the blood to drain welcomed back a wave of anxiety. Hagano sat down and fiddled with the box.

The top part twisted a few degrees. A piece on the side rattled in place. Clicks and scraping sounded as his fingers toyed with every surface. Nothing budged. A spark of anger lit inside him. What should have been an enjoyable gift did nothing more than annoy him.

Everything is a puzzle. Ecret's soft eyes smiled in his mind.

Hagano bounced his foot up and down, unable to control its agitation. *Don't think.*

The hole in the box put a ball in his stomach. Ecret was gone.

A box. A conversation.

Hagano clenched his jaw. The stubborn pieces lost all give.

It's time for me to go.

The muscles in his arms contracted. His foot bounced so fast it felt like vibrations. He exhaled slowly through his nose and let out a frustrated grunt. Lifting the box over his head, he slammed it down to the ground. A corner struck the dirt, cracking the wood. Hagano smashed the box again and again until it burst.

Splinters frayed out from the broken wood. Metallic tinks sounded. A white sparkle of light reflected off small pieces of metal on the ground—two silver coins and a small key. A string tied a curled piece of paper to the loop on the end. Hagano's breathing steadied. He grabbed the key and unfurled the note.

CAPHEO. SECTION 121. VOLUME II.

The word 'Capheo' had no meaning to him. What game was Alessi playing? 'Volume II' would indicate a specific book. 'Section 121' would then seem to point him to a spot in the temple library. But that section wasn't behind a locked door, so the key didn't make sense either. He frowned. The library sat deep inside the mountain temple —where he last saw The Sylph King. Whatever book Alessi wanted him to find was now unreachable.

"Hagano?!" The front door of the house slammed shut. "Hagano?!"

Alessi's voice made Hagano jump to his feet and run into the house. "Alessi." He wanted to smile, but felt frozen.

His brother's eyes found Hagano, making him nearly fall over as if a puppeteer had let go of his strings. He put a hand on his stomach. "You're okay?"

Hagano nodded. He stomped over to Alessi, reaching out with his good arm. The two embraced. Relief settled in Hagano's bones, keeping the need to pace around at bay. Part of the nightmare was over—his brother was safe. He could touch him and know for himself that Alessi was here, whole, and breathing. The hug felt awkward. The two rarely showed any affection, but Hagano didn't want to let go. For the first time since the attack, Hagano felt safe.

Alessi chuckled under his breath. "You stink."

A snort escaped Hagano's lips. "You're no daisy either."

They relaxed and let go of each other. The key in his sweaty palm slipped out and hit the floor.

Before Hagano could reach for it, Alessi bent over and picked it up. "What's this?"

Stupor struck Hagano. "It's the key."

Alessi unfurled the note. "The key to what?"

Hagano's brow tensed. "The key to... the one you put inside the puzzle box."

A confused frown smeared Alessi's face as he handed it over. "I didn't put a key in the puzzle box. Just some money."

The key sat on Hagano's open palm. His eyes glazed over as his mind raced. If Alessi didn't put the key in the box, who did? It had passed straight out of Alessi's hands into Hagano's. His eyes widened. That wasn't true. Ecret had examined the box. The key wasn't a gift from his brother, it was a gift from his god.

Closing his eyes, he could see Ecret tapping the box with a nail. *Every piece has its place.*

CHAPTER FIVE

MILENA

The family congregated around their table, each with a bowl of stew in front of them. The earthy aromas wafted up from steam. Carrots, potatoes, chicken, beans—all part of the family favorite meal, but the novelty held no appeal as Hagano's stomach clenched after the horrors of the day. He swirled his spoon in the bowl for the umpteenth time. Eating at a time like this felt stupid, but on a day brimming with uncertainty, routine prevailed.

Everyone sat quietly. Hagano kept his eyes off his parents to keep from looking at their sullen faces. He avoided Alessi too after they spent an hour disagreeing on the meaning of the key and the note. Hagano insisted Ecret wanted him to find that book regardless of what had happened. Alessi refused to believe that the god would put his brother in harm's way, choosing instead to believe that the box was somehow mixed up with another somewhere along the way.

"I should go." Alessi eyed the door but didn't move. A meeting of the remaining guards awaited him once night fell.

"It's not sunset yet." His mother folded her hands across her lap. "You still have a little time." She tried to smile, but the attempt only made her look sadder. "Both of you." She jutted her chin out at Hagano. "Just try to eat something."

Lifting the spoon to his lips, Hagano sipped at the stew. The familiar scent brought back feelings of holidays throughout his childhood—the joys of a new toy or the excitement of a new book. Every Day of Deliverance was just special enough for them to add chicken to the recipe. For a split second, he'd been transported to years past when everything was simple. Lord Ecret protected his people. Hagano wasn't managing a constant pain in his shoulder. His brother ran around the house with him, pretending to be guards fighting off imaginary trouble.

He swallowed a spoonful. The pungent broth tasted pleasant. Then a burnt flavor crossed his tongue. He chewed on whatever it was—discovering a piece of bitter chicken meat. He played with it in his mouth, wondering how boiled meat could taste so burnt. The only explanation he could muster was that a piece must have stuck to the side of the pot and crisped in the process. He took another spoonful. Everything tasted normal, save the meat—again.

"I liked Milena." His mother's comment was met by silence. Milena was always the most unpleasant of their chickens.

After a pause, his father offered a simple, "Why?"

"Yeah. Milena was an unusually mean bird." Hagano stared blankly at his food. His stomach protested the idea of ingesting any more of it.

"Well..." His mother paused to think for a moment. "She had grit."

His father leaned back, considering. "She was a chicken."

She pointed a finger up. "I know."

"A chicken that would peck you every chance she got," said Hagano.

"I know." She sipped her stew. "All I'm saying is that it's easy for a bear to have grit, but when a chicken's got grit, that's impressive."

Hagano and his father exchanged looks before nodding in unison.

Alessi gave no reaction, his mind elsewhere. "I should go." He stood. "Thank you for the meal."

"At least take some bread with you." His mother whisked herself to a box in the corner of the room and pulled out a loaf. "You barely touched your food."

"I'm fine." Alessi dismissed the bread with a wave of his hand.

Hagano's stomach knotted. He needed to get to the library and find that book. Ecret's conversation was like a puzzle, like he had said. Everything that had happened pointed to his god wanting Hagano to have that book. He knew it. Never in his life had he been so sure of something. He stood and locked eyes with his brother. "Let me go with you."

Alessi shook his head. "What? Hagano, no."

"Sit down, sweetie." His mother put her hand on Hagano's shoulder and tried to coax him back to his seat.

"The note and key are important and Ecret gave them to me." Hagano slipped out of his mother's grip.

"You don't know that." Alessi reached for the door.

"I do." Hagano stepped forward.

"We're not playing guards anymore, Hagano." Alessi's expression hardened. A fear filled his eyes. "You're injured. You didn't finish training. You can't help."

The words pierced Hagano, hitting him in his heart where he felt most vulnerable. But Ecret had given him his guard sword and told him he was practically retired. And he had given him a key and clues that would lead him to whatever knowledge that book contained. Nothing Alessi—or anyone—could say would take that away. "What if you're wrong?"

"Son, please." His father leaned forward in his chair. "Let Alessi handle this."

Hagano shook his head. "What if the key was part of something bigger? What if Ecret knew what was going to happen and the key was part of his plan?"

"Then what?" Alessi stood up straight and released his grip on the door handle. "You want to go *inside* the temple where The Sylph King is? You? An 18-year-old with a broken shoulder."

Hagano rolled his lips inward. He could feel a heat rising.

"How could I possibly entertain the idea of putting you in danger?" A softness returned to Alessi's face, relaxing his tense brow.

"Just let me go meet with the guards." His chances of finding that book felt like they were slipping out of reach.

"Hagano." His mother's soft voice tried to ease his nerves, but only sharpened them.

"All we're doing is discussing what we saw and heard during the attack so we can figure out what to do next." Alessi lifted his chin and sighed.

"Great. I was there." Hagano stepped forward. "I saw and heard things too. I can help."

A look of frustration flitted across Alessi's face. He'd played his cards wrong, giving Hagano a window to both go to the meeting and stay out of harm's way. "Look. Some of the guards heard The Sylph King say he was looking for the endling. So unless you know what the endling is—"

"I know what the endling is." Hagano clenched his fists in excitement. He wasn't lying about knowing, but would have if it would get him to that meeting. Years of delving into the depths of the library had equipped him with knowledge of ancient lore.

"What is it?" Alessi's shoulders slumped as he relaxed, clearly relieved that this knowledge would give the guards some sort of breakthrough.

Hagano paused. He could tell his brother now, but then he'd have to stay here and be stuck figuring out how to get to the temple library. His mind raced to find a solution that wouldn't anger his brother, but came up empty. "I'll tell you at the meeting."

Alessi squinted. He folded his arms. "Fine."

CHAPTER SIX

THE SAFE HOUSE

The full moon peeked through the clouds, casting light on the city streets. Hagano and Alessi stood outside the most boring home Hagano had ever seen. The clay walls and wooden frame looked exactly like every other house. Black curtains hung inside. Nothing distinguished it from anywhere else—no plants, no porch, nothing. If Hagano didn't known better, he would have assumed the place was vacant. But here they were—at the supposed rendezvous point. He hummed to himself. *So this is what a safe house looks like.*

Alessi stepped in front of his brother. "You're here to share what you saw during the attack and…" He rolled his eyes. "Explain what an endling is. Then you're going straight home. Got it?" His eyes squinted at the end of his thought.

"Right." Hagano flashed his teeth in a grin.

"Don't bring up the key." Alessi prodded Hagano's chest with a finger. "I don't want anyone distracted by *anything* right now. We need to focus."

"I got it." Hagano threw up his hands as if to surrender. "I heard you the first twelve times."

The trek to this house passed mostly in silence, save Alessi warning Hagano not to talk about the key from Ecret. Hagano would have objected, but didn't want to give his brother any reason to change his mind about letting him tag along. One looming thought occupied him during the walk—should he tell Alessi about the strange vision he'd had? It sounded crazy the more he thought about it. A fish in a hand and voice telling him to eat? And all of that happened during some sort of out-of-body experience. Maybe it was all in his head caused by shock and trauma. That would only make Alessi worry more and that was the last thing Hagano needed right now. What was important was getting to the book—somehow.

Lifting a fist to the door, Alessi stopped and spun back to Hagano. "Please." He clapped his hands together as if in prayer. "Listen to me. The Hallux is missing. Most of the guards, including the high-ranking ones, were killed at the festival." A long, breathy sigh seeped out of his teeth. "I am doing my best to follow orders, keep the faith, and figure out what we can do from here. I *really* don't need you going off script and making things harder." His face tightened, looking like he was bracing himself to lift the weight of the world.

"Okay." Hagano rocked back and forth.

Three raps at the door cued the sound of footsteps from the other side. The door creaked open.

"It's Captain Alessi."

Captain? Hagano tilted his head. His brother wasn't exaggerating —the higher ups must have all died in order for someone so young to get such a promotion.

The door swung open and a woman waved them inside.

She looked familiar, middle-aged, strong. Something clicked, sparking the memory of the woman who sat next to Hagano before the attack. What was her name? Jana? Juna?

"Well, this is a surprise." She lifted her chin as she looked Hagano up and down. "Glad to see you in one piece, Hagano." Her wooden staff leaned against the wall behind her.

"Yes, hi." He chewed on his bottom lip. Of course, she remembered his name and he couldn't recall hers.

"It's Jaga." She winked. Something had given away his forgetfulness—probably a panicked look Hagano was unaware he was making.

Alessi surveyed the room. "Hagano knows what the endling is, so I brought him along to explain."

"Very well." Jaga closed the door. Her tawny skin and black hair seemed unusually pristine considering the events of the day.

The interior of the place was as empty and unremarkable as it looked on the outside. The house consisted of a spacious guest area and a door leading to what Hagano assumed was a bedroom. A handful of chairs furnished the home. Nothing hung on the walls. A few scattered candles brought a touch of light to the space. Several guards filled the room looking grim-faced and weary.

Hagano found himself retreating against a wall as everyone sized him up. He turned to Jaga. "You have a lovely place."

She lifted a brow. "Do you think I live here?"

"Uh." He tried to force a laugh. "I was just... kidding."

Alessi stepped between Jaga and his brother. "Is this everyone?"

Her lips tightened as she gave a curt nod.

Hagano scanned the room to count the guards. Ten, including Alessi. That's all. Three of them displayed fresh bandages on their arms or legs. One looked like he could barely sit up straight as he slouched in a chair against the far wall.

Where were the hundreds of guards the city employed? Hagano had seen them mere hours ago. He fought back a sense of dread. Some had been killed, but how many? A lot? Most? Yes—that's what Alessi said outside. Most. Who did that leave? A small portion of survivors, some of which must be seriously injured and tending to their wounds. That left only ten?

Trepidation crept over his skin. Did some of them abandon their post and flee the battle? Had they forsaken their oath? Where were they now? He could see the image of a guard, sitting in the dark, his sword in hand, too ashamed to answer the call of his superiors. Would Hagano have been such a guard if he finished training? The thought put goosebumps on his arms.

A new worry made his palms sweat. Ecret's great peace might now be to their disadvantage. War had become a relic of history when Ecret defeated The Sylph King six hundred years ago. Dozens of generations had passed since anyone had seen battle. Everyone who now lived had no more experience with an enemy than Hagano. The worst fight anyone standing in this room had was probably with a sparring partner.

He patted his pocket. The small bump of the key settled the sting of his nerves. It was a message—a sign that Ecret was still helping them from beyond the grave. He just didn't know what the message was yet.

Alessi walked to the center of the room. "Everyone, thank you for coming. As you can see, we are few in number."

"This is all that's coming?" A brawny woman pulled a pipe from her mouth. "What are we supposed to do?"

Everyone fidgeted where they stood.

"I don't know yet." Alessi straightened his posture. "We know The Sylph King is looking for something called the endling."

"What is that?" Another guard cleared his throat.

"I've brought someone who can explain." Alessi's eyes bore down on Hagano as if to remind him once again to not bring up the key.

Hagano tapped his pocket and stepped forward. "It's uh..." His mouth dried. The air tasted stale. He cleared his throat. "It's an epithet."

No one moved.

The guard with the pipe blew a puff of smoke from her lips. "Are we supposed to know what that is too?"

"Oh." Hagano wiped his palms on his pants. "It's like a title. You know... like..." He wrapped his bad arm around his ribs. "Ecret, the Psychopomp. All the gods had them, anciently, before the division. Since Ecret ferries people to the afterlife, he is—was—a psychopomp. So his title describes him." He shrugged his good shoulder.

Alessi's brow furrowed. "And?"

Hagano swallowed hard, somehow feeling like a rock went down his throat. "An endling is a creature that is the last of its species. The first god is The Primogenitor and the fifth and final one is Inturon... the endling." Whatever book had given him this piece of knowledge, he couldn't quite remember, but he was sure this information was indeed fact.

"Inturon?" Jaga leaned against her staff. "The bearcat god hasn't set foot in Ecretia in over six hundred years." A skepticism coated her words.

Everyone nodded in agreement.

A cloud of smoke blew from a guard's lips. She focused on Jaga. "And we're just supposed to believe a kid? How does he even know any of this?"

Shrugging a shoulder, Hagano looked to the floor. "Books."

"He's something of a historian." Alessi cleared his throat.

The word 'historian' made Hagano's back stiff. The word was generous, but seemed to afford Hagano some credit. "Yeah." He mouthed 'thank you' to Alessi before turning to the group. "Inturon is the endling and one of Lord Ecret's brothers."

"Alright." Another puff of smoke shrouded the gruff guard. "So we contact this other god and hope he can kill The Sylph King."

"It'll be months before they get back to us. Inturon's home city is terribly far." Jaga rocked on her heels and shook her head.

"We'll send an envoy—tonight." Alessi pointed to a pair. "Ready some horses. You leave in an hour."

"Inturon could be *here*." The words escaped Hagano before he had a chance to stop them. His head suddenly felt as heavy as a boulder.

"Again." Jaga rubbed her temple. "Inturon hasn't set foot in Ecretia for six hundred years."

"I know." Hagano tapped the key in his pocket. He tried to look at Jaga, but his eyes flitted away from her stare. "But The Sylph King went *inside* The Mountain Temple. If Inturon is out there—" He pointed in the direction he thought was West. "Then The Sylph King went the wrong way."

"You think Inturon is inside the temple?" One of the guards chimed up, but Hagano couldn't tell which.

He relaxed his shoulders and let out a deep breath. "I think that if The Sylph King is looking for Inturon inside the temple, our best chance is looking in the same place."

Jaga's expression changed to almost a proud grin.

Alessi stepped to Hagano's side and leaned close. "Please tell me this is not an attempt to go after that book."

"Also, Ecret wants us to find a book." Hagano froze, waiting for Alessi to snap, but he had to say it. This is what his god wanted and no one—not his brother, not the guards, not The Sylph King—could scare him into keeping quiet.

Alessi let out a gravelly moan.

"Santora. Section five. Volume four." The woman put down her pipe and lifted a small key in the air. A small note dangled from it. "That book?"

Alessi and Hagano exchanged confused glances.

Reaching into his pocket, Hagano produced his key. "No. Capheo. Section one-twenty-one. Volume two."

The feeble guard in the corner pushed himself up and lifted a key in the air. "Aumenia. Section forty-five. Volume one."

Alessi buried his face in his hands. He exhaled through gritted teeth and pushed back his hair. Turning to Hagano, he narrowed his eyes. Something about his stare made him look like he would collapse at any moment. "It's settled then. We're going back to the temple."

CHAPTER SEVEN

JUST ONE STEP

Eight of the guards split into two teams and left the safehouse ten minutes apart. Alessi had instructed them to make their way to their designated section of the library and rendezvous at some place called 'safehouse five'. Hagano wondered what number safehouse he was standing in, but didn't ask. His brother had barely looked him in the eyes since deciding they needed to go back to the temple. By Hagano's estimate, they had roughly eight hours until sunrise and their rendezvous time. It would take half an hour to reach the temple. If they were walking straight from the front door to the library entrance deep inside the mountain, that would be another ten minutes. But the plan was to use the back tunnels and winding halls. Who knew how long that would take?

Alessi's hands darted back and forth as he whispered to Jaga in the corner.

Hagano couldn't hear, but assumed Alessi's frantic expressions and Jaga's reassuring nods meant that Alessi wasn't happy about Hagano tagging along. He brushed his fingers over his sling, lightly rubbing his aching arm. *Capheo. What are you? Who are you?* Two thoughts prevailed—Capheo was either the author of the book Ecret wanted him to have or Capheo was something inside the book Hagano needed to understand.

The garbled whispering stopped. Alessi walked over to the door of what Hagano assumed was a bedroom and unlocked it. "Hagano, grab a candle. We need to get dressed and get on our way."

"Hm?" Hagano's focus returned to his surroundings. "Dressed?" He picked up the nearest candelabra and followed Alessi into the secondary room.

A wall of weapons greeted him. Swords, staffs, maces, scimitars, and a dozen other blades he couldn't name decorated the walls. Large straw baskets lined the floor. Alessi pointed to them. "Help me find some black clothing for the both of us."

Hagano set down the candles, close enough for the flames to illuminate the baskets, but far enough to not catch anything on fire. Lifting a lid, he pulled out a green robe with golden accents—something he'd never once seen on the streets of the temple city. Another scoop of clothing revealed a thin, silver crown with beads hanging off opposite sides. "What is all this stuff?"

Alessi tipped over a near empty basket and rifled through its contents. "Supplies."

"For what?" Hagano tossed a leather cowl to the side.

"Blending in."

Hagano almost laughed at the thought. "Blending in? Where?"

Clearing his throat, Alessi opened another basket. "Everywhere that isn't here. Inturon's kingdom. The other gods' kingdoms."

"Uh..." Hagano peeked inside a bag at a collection of strange golden jewelry. "That doesn't make sense. The borders are closed."

"Officially, yes." Alessi pulled out a black shirt and held it up to his chest.

"And unofficially?" Hagano leaned away from his brother. He knew the answer already. The evidence was in his hands. Something dug into him, but he couldn't quite tell what it was. Was he bothered that Alessi kept this information from him? Or was he more disturbed that a long-held belief was wrong? Had Ecret been lying? Hagano shook his head. No. It must be more complicated than that.

"This looks like it will fit you. Put it on." Alessi tossed Hagano a clump of black clothes.

The two shed their white festival outfits and replaced them with plain, black garments. Hagano tucked the key into his pocket.

"Take a sword." Alessi grabbed one for himself and left the room.

A strange sense of darkness crept up on Hagano. He rubbed his thumb back and forth across his fingers. Candlelight flickered across the metallic blades. His eyes scanned each of them, thinking that one of the weapons would speak to him. None were the type of sword he had grown accustomed to and he hadn't trained in much else beyond a guard's standard issue. At one point he wanted to learn the broadsword, but the horse kick to his shoulder killed that dream.

He lifted a scimitar off the wall. It felt light enough to manage, but wasn't sure how the curve would affect a swing of the blade. Flicking his wrist, he tested its movements. With a few practice strikes, the scimitar felt like it almost floated through the air. Grabbing the sheath, he attached it to his waist. Pausing, he let in a deep breath and exhaled slowly. In a few short hours, he'd gone from believing all was lost to holding the future of his country in his hands. Everything rested on the path his key would take him on. Walking out of this room would be the first step.

His feet wouldn't move. A prickling under his skin spread over his body as if every facet of his being told him to hold back. Stop. Wait. Run away. The path to the library led only to death. The Sylph King stood in his way.

Just take one step. That's it. Just one. He closed his eyes and took a step. *Good. Now you've already started. Just keep going.* Hagano entered the foyer.

Alessi leaned against the door. "You ready?"

With a nod, Hagano accompanied his brother outside. "Where's Jaga?"

"She left." With a twist of a key, Alessi locked the door. "Thought it was better if she worked on her own."

A grumbling in Hagano's gut didn't buy it. Jaga must have gone by herself because she thought sticking with Hagano was nothing more than babysitting—or worse, a death sentence.

"Stay close. Keep quiet, even out here." Alessi rested his hand on the hilt of his sword. "We don't know the enemies' movements. I'll take us through some backstreets until we reach the southern side of the temple. I assume you can take us on a safe path to the library from there."

Hagano nodded and whispered a short, "Yes." Never before did he think that his familiarity with the library would put him in a life or death situation—for him or his brother.

"Just so we're clear..." Alessi's jaw flinched. "If we happen upon one of the sylphs or even The Sylph King, don't engage."

"Then what do we do?"

"We run." A twitch in his eyes hinted at some deeper thought Alessi wasn't sharing. "I want you at least ten feet behind me at all times. When I do this—" He held up his hand, his thumb in front of his palm. "You stop. This means run." He pointed two fingers downward.

"I remember the hand signals." The reminders made Hagano want to roll his eyes. It had only been three months since his expulsion from training and here Alessi was acting like Hagano was a new recruit.

"Good. It's just the two of us so we can move more stealthily as a smaller unit. Stick to the shadows." He reached for Hagano's shoulder but stopped short and put down his hand. "You ready?"

"Eat." A deep voice behind Hagano pierced him.

He whipped his neck around, but saw no one. A slight breeze tickled his ears. Moonlight cast shadows on the street.

"What is it?" Alessi tensed.

"Nothing." A hint of burnt meat on his tongue fought for Hagano's attention. He blinked repeatedly, forcing himself to focus on Alessi. "It's nothing."

"You sure?" Alessi held his breath.

Hagano forced a smile and nodded.

"Okay." Alessi exhaled. "Remember, ten feet." He turned to leave. "Let's go."

CHAPTER EIGHT

SPILT BLOOD

Backstreets and shadows comprised the path back to the temple. The closer Alessi and Hagano got, the more his heart raced. He couldn't guess how long they'd spent walking, stopping, waiting, and walking again on repeat as Alessi checked for enemies around every corner.

The stillness of the night sat lopsided in Hagano's stomach. For a city populated by millions of people, the whispering of a breeze was somehow the loudest sound.

As far as Hagano could tell, they were heading towards the main gate, but avoiding the main road. Abandoned festival stands littered the streets, their merchandise left for anyone to take freely. Toys, decorations, and souvenirs lay scattered about. Homes and businesses displayed no sign of life—no light nor sound coming from any of them.

"Can I ask you something?" A nagging thought had lingered in the back of Hagano's mind long enough.

Alessi responded with a sharp 'shh'.

"I'm just very confused about something—the woman—the one with the face like a cheetah. Who was she?"

"I don't know." Alessi put a finger to his lips and glared. Stopping at a corner, he held out a small mirror to peek down the adjacent street.

Following a wave of Alessi's hand, Hagano jogged across the cobblestones and into the shadows. "Why would any person help The Sylph King? What could she possibly gain?"

A sulking Alessi waited for him. Leaning close, the few inches Alessi had on him felt more towering than ever. "Hagano, stop talking."

"But—"

"None of us know who she is or why she's helping The Sylph King." Alessi pushed out his cheek with his tongue and exhaled through his nose. "I get the temptation to think out loud and sort it out, but now's not the time. Focus. We have a mission. Travelling unnoticed is our only priority until we reach the library." He turned about and picked up a brisk pace.

Hagano lowered his head and whispered, "Sorry."

The rhythmic jogging eased Hagano's whirlwind of thought, channeling the words in his head into one idea. Six centuries ago, Ecret claimed this land with the help of The Seven Saints. Each saint possessed a supernatural gift. These abilities, bestowed by Lord Ecret himself, gave them a power no normal person could otherwise possess. With those powers, they defeated The Sylph King and his forces. Now this cheetah-faced woman possessed a power like one of The Seven Saints. Her blood ate through skin and stone. She could control it, sending it moving around in the air as if it was an extra limb. And somehow, that same acidic blood existed in the bodies of the attacking sylphs. But history taught that The Sylph King did not share his power. His greed and ego were too great. So where did the cheetah-faced woman's abilities come from?

The two reached the end of the housing blocks. Piles of rubble stood where homes had been just that morning. Proximity to the temple was once the most coveted possession in the entire country. Now it seemed the opposite.

Alessi ducked behind a wall. Using his mirror, he peered around the corner at the temple courtyard, then back at Hagano. Alessi waved to him, whispering, "We're almost there. From here on out, I need you to be silent."

"I thought I was being silent."

"You're stepping loudly, you're breathing loudly, and your sword has been slapping against your leg."

Hagano shrugged. "Sorry. I'll try to breathe more *quietly*."

"Just stay close. Stay behind me. Stay quiet. And if I tell you to run, you leave me behind and run as fast as you can."

Hagano blanched. Running away meant deserting not only his brother, but also his protection. At least he had confidence in his ability to run. His speed, after all, was one of the main reasons he was able to find work as a courier. Despite the ball in his stomach, Hagano nodded an agreement.

Alessi peered around the corner towards the temple again. His focus stayed fixed for so long that Hagano's legs began to feel jittery.

Hagano swayed back and forth. "What is it?"

"See for yourself." Alessi switched places with him and passed the mirror. "Look at the temple gates."

It took a minute for Hagano to wobble his wrist in just the right direction for the reflection to find what he was looking for. He squinted.

Ecret's body hung upside down at the temple gates. A flurry of sylphs scurried around the dead god. It looked as if one of them was hammering a nail into Ecret's talons. A few more held up the body as the wings fell to Ecret's side. The image of the dead god didn't feel real—but stung all the same. Hagano tightened his squeeze on the mirror, maneuvering it every which way. Grunting, he used it make sure the road was empty and poked his head out to survey the scene without the hassle.

"Hey." Alessi tugged on Hagano's arms.

Rolling his shoulder out of Alessi's grasp, he pulled back just far enough that he could still look down the road with one eye. "The road's clear."

"For now," Alessi whispered.

A brutish man in festival clothing sauntered up to Ecret's

dangling head. With a slice of a sword, congealed blood oozed from Ecret's neck.

Hagano leaned back to Alessi. "They slit his throat."

"Hmmm?" Alessi snatched the mirror and crouched down to see. "Why spill his blood? He's already dead."

Something nagged at Hagano like a thought that refused to form. Click—two ideas merged. An image of Milena hanging on the nail back home flashed before his eyes. "Maybe they're not spilling it. Maybe they're draining it."

"Why?" Alessi adjusted his squat.

The answer felt obvious, but he didn't want to jump to conclusions. The cheetah-faced woman's power was blood based. Now they were collecting not just blood, but god-blood.

The sight of Ecret brought his words back to Hagano. *Everything is a puzzle.*

His heart sank. Maybe the vision of the fish and voice telling him to eat were not messages. Maybe they were Ecret's dying words—not his dying wish. Maybe everything Hagano saw and felt was a god's version of flapping its wings after its head had been severed.

"We should keep moving." Alessi stood and glanced up and down the street.

"Okay."

Another hour brought them to the southern walls that merged into the mountainside. The full moon shone brightly, creating harsh shadows in which they could hide. Ancient trees decorated the temple grounds, offering additional cover. After crawling up a handful of levels, the two reached a door.

Alessi pressed his ear against the wood. Only the breeze and the chattering of nocturnal insects surrounded them. With a nod, Alessi jerked the door open. The metal hinges creaked.

Hagano winced at the sound and waited to see if the noise attracted anyone.

No one came.

The two slipped inside.

CHAPTER NINE

EVENING. RATS.

The temple halls grew darker as Hagano and Alessi ventured deeper into the belly of the mountain. Moonlight from scattered windows illuminated less and less of their path. None of the torches at hallway intersections were lit, leaving them at times in complete darkness.

The sound of Alessi's footsteps stopped in a place that offered no light. "Hagano."

"Hm?" The pause in their movements gave Hagano goosebumps. Had Alessi heard something?

"We need new signals." The rattling of a pebble echoed right next to them, presumably kicked by Alessi's foot. "We're safest in the darkness where the hand signals won't work. Let's switch to verbal."

"Okay." Something kept Hagano from remembering the standard verbal cues taught to him in training. Hand signals were always preferred, so the verbal ones were far less practiced. "What are they again?" He took his hand off the wall—his only guide in the lightless tunnel.

"Stop, forward, left, right, and back go like this." Alessi made a series of noises that sounded like half-whistles and half-clicks. After a beat, he repeated himself. "Now you do it."

Hagano tried, but the noises were so odd even he could tell he wasn't getting them right.

"Close enough." Another stone rattled around on the floor. "If we confront an enemy, I won't use the sounds. Don't want to tip them off that I'm signaling someone else."

Hagano started to nod, but realized Alessi couldn't see him. "Okay."

"If we run into an enemy, we must first try not to engage. But if I say the word 'evening', then I want you to attack. It'll mean I see only one enemy and I think you'll be able to get the jump on him. Do the same for me. But if I say the word 'rat' or 'rats', I want you to stay hidden and continue on without me."

"But—" Hagano pulled the arm in his sling closer to him.

"You can do this, Hagano."

His brother's reassurance stilled Hagano. At no point between the attack and now had Alessi given any show of faith in his brother. Those five words—*You can do this, Hagano*—filled him with the same warmth and comfort that Lord Ecret's did. They settled Hagano's nerves and bolstered his spirit. Yet, lurking behind them sat a twinge of fear. Did Alessi already believe they would be separated? Had he already made the choice to sacrifice himself so Hagano would have a chance to find the book and fulfill Ecret's wishes?

"Let's keep moving." Alessi's tone sobered.

"Okay." Hagano put his hand back on the wall and followed the sounds of Alessi's whistles and clicks.

After winding through a countless series of halls, a pale light shone down from above a staircase. The steps faded into the darkness below and grew more visible as they moved upward.

Alessi muttered something under his breath. "Do you know which way to go?"

"Umm." Hagano looked down the halls and up the stairs. "No. I'm completely turned around."

"Me too." Alessi frowned.

A flickering, red light appeared in an adjacent hall. With the light came a voice singing in a foreign tongue.

Alessi whistled a signal, but Hagano dashed down the stairwell without realizing which direction he was supposed to go. His heart drummed like thunder, sending a throbbing pulse through his aching arm. Sweat coated his palms. He stepped lightly, hoping the sounds of his feet and the clinking of his sheath would go unnoticed. Stair after stair flew underfoot until he reached the next level and total darkness. He pressed his lips shut and pushed himself against a wall. His chest shivered as he tried to suppress the sound of heavy breathing.

The thumping in his ears made it harder to hear the notes of the strange song. Hagano's eyes shot open. He hadn't realized how tightly he'd been holding them shut. Where was Alessi? Reaching his hand to his side, he waved it around in search of anything that might orient him. His palm nicked the wall. Something dislodged and made a thud. He froze.

The amber light flickered above. The song continued—slowly, softly—like a lullaby.

Hagano reached for the hilt of his sword. He couldn't tell if the sylph was getting closer or farther. Did he need to fight? Did the creature hear the thud? As quietly as he could, Hagano curled his tongue to whistle, hoping that somehow Alessi would hear the sound and know where to find him. He took in a small breath, his jaw trembling.

"Looks like I've stumbled upon a rat." Alessi's voice echoed down the stairs.

Hagano's heart dropped to the floor. *Rat.* He wanted to scream and cry and fight and hide all at the same time. This couldn't be happening. Alessi couldn't have given him the signal to move on alone.

"Says the greasy creature scuttling around in the dark." The vowels in the sylph's voice sounded soft—a far cry from the guttural, scratchy voice Hagano always imagined a sylph would have.

"I guess we're both rats then."

Heavy footsteps thumped above. Another set started pounding not a second later. The light of the torch in the stairwell vanished.

Please! No! Please! Ecret! A desperate prayer of disjointed words stormed inside Hagano. He dashed up the stairs, tripping at the top when his foot reached for a step that wasn't there. Fumbling, his feet flailed, but kept him from falling. Distant footsteps echoed to his left and straight on, but he couldn't tell which way Alessi fled.

He was gone. Hagano was alone.

The cold air met the sweat on his back. It almost stung. He panted.

The sound of footsteps ceased.

Hagano covered his mouth with one hand. Nervous tears pooled in his eyes.

Eternity seemed to pass as he waited for something to happen. Would Alessi return? Would another sylph appear? Would something give him even the smallest sense of direction and start him on the path to the library? The soft whisper of the wind drifted in the air. Moonlight vanished from the stairwell as a cloud blocked it out as it passed through the sky.

"Alessi?" whispered Hagano, not expecting a reply. But if the torchlight was gone, then so was the sylph. That didn't mean Alessi couldn't have escaped his pursuer and made his way back. While small, the chance for them to meet up was worth at least a whisper. "Are you there?"

No response.

He walked up to another level and whispered once again.

Nothing. Time to keep moving. How could Hagano have been so stupid? If only he'd paid attention to which signal Alessi had given— he would have never run in the wrong direction and left his brother's side.

Ecret? If you are still out there and can hear me, please help Alessi.

The halls grew colder as Hagano moved closer to the heart of the temple. The last of the fresh air turned musty, leaving a stale taste on his tongue. After many guesses as to which path to take and several dead ends, Hagano found a part of the temple that looked at least somewhat familiar. He leaned against the wall of a balcony. A cavern opened up before him, circled by six levels that all looked down at a lobby filled with historical artifacts.

By his guess, it would take him at least half an hour to walk around the entirety of the room. Hagano inched his way to the edge of the balcony and looked over to get a sense of where he was. A suit of armor caught his eye. The feathers that decorated it sparked his memory—this was the gallery of The Seven Saints. He scanned the room, glancing at every part lit up by the moonlight reflected off a series of mirrors. His shoulders went limp from the relief of seeing this place. It fed directly into the library.

Hagano pulled his weak arm to his ribs and took hold of his sheath with his good hand. Beelining for the entrance, he ran with all his strength. Sweat dripped from his hairline. He tapped his pocket, checking to make sure the key was still there. The small lump greeted his fingers.

His energy lasted just short of the library entrance. Soreness in his legs snuck up on him. Fatigue weighed down his head. He'd been awake for nearly a day and the adrenaline in his veins was losing its effect.

A sign at the door welcomed him to the Grand Library. It pointed to 'Level 2, Sections 51 through 100'. His destination was still one floor up, but now he knew exactly where he was and how to get there. He turned his ear to the empty chambers and closed his eyes, hoping that no sound would alarm him. The stairs to the next level weren't far and he could stick to the outer wall.

A glimmer shone from the opposite side of library. It flickered red.

Hagano's stomach tangled into a knot. Someone was here. He slid behind a bookcase and crouched. Peeking between shelves, he watched the light strengthen. Whoever held the distant torch was still not visible, but he had no doubt it was a sylph.

The orange glow erupted into a wall of flame. Darkness gave way to a hungry fire as it devoured books and shelves. Light and heat enveloped the room.

Hagano swallowed the lump in his throat. His favorite place in the world was now up in flames. Pages of history were vanishing by the second. The Sylph King must have known about the keys and sent someone to stop Ecret's plan. Hagano would have to outrace the fire —without being seen.

CHAPTER TEN

FIRE

The path to Section 121 of the library drew itself in Hagano's mind. He dashed down an aisle, sticking close to the outer wall and as far away from the gorging flames as he possibly could. He turned left, then right. Sizzling, warm light spread—threatening to blind him as his eyes adjusted from the darkness. The taste of smoke reached his tongue. Another left. Straight through. Aisle after aisle passed with no sign of an enemy. The patter of his feet felt louder than ever despite his efforts to step lightly.

He turned right. The stairwell came into view. A burst of adrenaline hit his veins. His pace doubled.

The crackling of wood broke through the air. The heat bore down on him. The fire grew closer as if it were racing him to the stairwell.

His shoulder throbbed. His arm ached. He coughed.

Ashes floated in the air. The smoke gagged him.

He bounded for the first steps, his eyes darting every which way in case someone was close. He heaved, steps passing underfoot three at a time. The stairs spiraled and opened to the next level.

More smoke clouded the air. He crouched, trying to sink below its noxious hold. From across the room, the light of the fire sparked, beginning the second course of its bounteous feast.

A sign above him read 'Section 100'. Hagano clenched his teeth and grunted. The fire was at the opposite side and the book was in the middle. He'd have to reach it before the flames. There was no time to hide his movement.

Hunched over, he sped across the room holding the collar of his shirt over his nose and mouth. *Please let me get to it first!*

He tried to not think about what would happen if he failed, but the thoughts barged in unwelcomed. Had Alessi sacrificed himself for nothing? Did Ecret trust Hagano with a puzzle he'd failed to solve? Would The Sylph King reign over his people and their souls for eternity? Did everything count on him running faster than a fire?

His eyes stung. Tears tried to clear his vision as he blinked, but everything turned foggy. Section 111 passed, then 113. He coughed. Burning shelves collapsed, sending more smoke and ash in every direction.

Sucking in a breath, he straightened his back and ran full speed to his appointed section. Air left his nostrils in bursts, exhausting his supply faster than he hoped.

Section 121 arrived. He turned. The fire loomed only a handful of aisles away. Running his fingers along the wall of books, his eyes scanned for the word 'Capheo'. Glancing down the length of the section, no bars blocked off any shelf. Whatever the key was for, it wasn't to get to the book. Soot fell on his tongue. He spat and wheezed, but the smoke in the air kept him from catching his breath.

Hagano squatted, choking and fighting for breath. He knelt down and put his nose to the floor. The air on the ground was still cool and clean—enough for his head to clear. He crawled down the aisle, glancing up until reaching the case where his book should be.

The crackling of flames grew louder. A wave of heat hit him.

His heart thumping, he scanned the spines of the books. *Callion. Calpen. Caonu. Capheo.* He jolted upright and reached for the book —*Capheo, Volume 1.* His mind blanked. Wrong volume. But which volume was it? His heart drummed. He couldn't remember. *Volume 2!* He reached for the next book, but the spine read 'Volume 5'. His stomach twisted. It wasn't here. He'd come all this way and the book wasn't here. *No!* He ran his fingers over every book in front of him. It had to be here—someone must have misplaced it.

The salty sting of sweat hit his eyes. Fire tore into the shelves on the other side of him. A wall of light lit up his face. He squinted, but kept searching. The flames would reach him in seconds, and the book had to be here. Lord Ecret sent him here and he would have only done that if the book was here. He blinked rapidly. Volume 6. Volume 8. Volume 12. Volume 2. There it was! He jerked the book from its brothers and sprinted away from the inferno.

Smoke scratched his throat, but the air cleared as he put more distance between him and the fire. His cough slowed his run, but he felt like he could sprint for miles. He'd succeeded and with any luck, so had the others. The third level library entrance drew close. His legs slowed. His stamina withered, but he'd made it. The cavernous chamber opened up as he exited the library and jogged toward the nearest dark hallway.

Crumbling to the floor, he leaned his head against the wall and held the book to his chest. Through panted breaths, the world calmed. His body relaxed. His heartbeat quieted.

"And who might you be?"

The voice sent chills down Hagano's spine. He froze.

A man about Hagano's age stepped out of the shadows. Blocks of black ink painted his eyes and cheekbones, with smears of white above and below them—making him look like a raccoon. The glowing light of the fire glinted off the rapier in his hand.

CHAPTER ELEVEN

LOWELL'S GIFT

T he racoon-faced sylph relaxed his posture. He sheathed his rapier. Something about Hagano's appearance must have put him at ease.

A flood of incoherent thoughts fought for center stage in Hagano's mind. He couldn't tell the truth about who he was and what he was doing, but what lie would save him? *Say something. Anything. Just start talking.*

"What are you holding?" The sylph pointed at the book Hagano pressed against his chest.

"I need your help." Hagano swallowed hard.

The light of the fire grew, dispelling the darkness around the sylph. Something about him felt like the guards he trained with—his stoic demeanor, his athletic build, his hint of cockiness.

"You need help?" The sylph cocked his head to the side.

"Yes." Fighting every urge to melt, Hagano pushed himself to his feet. "The Sylph King attacked during the festival." Images of the attack flashed in his mind, pricking like needles. "I ran and hid in the library and have been waiting there all day for someone to come along. I don't know what happened, but then it caught on fire." He tried to steady his shaking hands, but couldn't.

"Is that so?" The corners of the sylph's lips turned upward.

"Yes." Hagano looked into his eyes, trying to read the sylph's intentions.

A deadpan expression offered no insight. "Give me the book."

Hagano squeezed it tighter. "You want my book?"

"Yes." The sylph extended a hand.

Don't engage. Alessi's warnings crawled under Hagano's skin. But he couldn't give up the book, not before he had the chance to learn its contents. He'd have to make a run for it and lose the sylph in the maze of the temple hallways. But the fire robbed Hagano of the darkness he so desperately needed. Its light spread in every direction.

Maybe his panic was premature. The sylph couldn't have known what was in the book. Perhaps he wanted to check to see if it was worth burning and hand it right back. Hagano forced a smile. He couldn't risk it. If the book left his hands, it might never come back.

The sylph stepped forward and grabbed the top of the book. "Give it here." He clenched his jaw and tugged at it.

Hagano snapped it closer to him, fighting the sylph's pull.

The sylph reached with both hands.

Time slowed. Hagano had but a second to fend off the sylph. With only one good hand, he'd never be able outmuscle his enemy. He threw his knee into the sylph's crotch.

A pained breath escaped his lips as he doubled over.

Hagano ran.

The heat of the fire sizzled on his skin as he sped past the library entrance. Smoke floated out of the doorway, rising up through the cavern. His tired muscles begged for rest, but he had to run with every ounce of strength still left inside him. He needed to find somewhere safe to read. Warm sweat dripped down his back. He took in a deep breath and lengthened his stride. Lifting his foot, for the briefest of moments, he felt like he could fly.

Flickering orange light revealed a stairwell only seconds away at his current pace. If he could reach it, he might be free. A burst of sharp pain exploded in his shoulder. *Just keep running.*

The book began to slip from his sweating palms. He tucked it under his armpit. The waist of his pants loosened. The fit of the borrowed clothes poorer than his own. *The clothes!* Hagano wanted to scream at himself. That's why the sylph didn't believe Hagano's lie. If he had truly run from the festival to the library, he would have been wearing traditional white, not black. What a dumb mistake.

The staircase neared. No sounds of footsteps echoed behind him, but he dared not look back. *Almost...there.* His body wavered back and forth as he ran unevenly, but his escape was but a few yards away. *Just ten more seconds.* His muscles protested, nearly sapped of all strength. *You can run just ten more seconds.* He pushed harder against the ground, forcing himself to increase his efforts. *Nine more seconds... Eight more—*

The world shifted in the blink of an eye. A buzzing hit his ear. The sight of the staircase turned into the sight of the sylph—far away —running toward that same staircase. A thud sounded next to him. He looked down—the book had fallen. His hands held his groin. His bad arm had slipped from his sling.

The sylph across the room fumbled to a stop. He turned around, one hand pressed against his crotch. Limping, the sylph started walking back.

Hagano's eyes narrowed. They'd switched places. But how? Did this raccoon-faced sylph also possess a power? No other explanation presented itself. The thumping in his chest began to hurt. He tucked his bad arm back into the sling. A tingling crept up his neck. He'd nowhere to run and nowhere to hide. The sylph would be back in less than a minute.

"Hey!" A female voice shouted from below. "Leave him alone."

Picking up the book, Hagano rushed to the balcony railing.

Jaga stood on the second floor, wooden staff in hand. She extended it, pointing it at the sylph. "That boy isn't the one you should be worried about."

The sylph spat on the ground, his limp waning as he closed in on Hagano.

His pulse drummed in his ears. Could he thumb through the book before the sylph arrived? He tsked. No. The risk was too high. If he failed, the sylph would seize it and all would be lost. The best thing he could do was try and save the book. Like Alessi, he'd have to sacrifice himself. "Jaga!"

Her eyes met Hagano's.

"I have the book. Take it and go." He threw it over the balcony.

She reached out her arms.

But the book landed in the hands of the sylph—not Jaga's.

Hagano looked to his side. Jaga now stood where the sylph had been. Now they had switched places.

"Thank you." The sylph shrugged and tossed the book into the burning library. "All too easy."

"No!" Hagano's body shook as he screamed.

Jaga flew over the edge of the balcony. Rolling across the floor, she recovered in an instant. She charged toward the sylph and swung her staff at his head.

Something buzzed. An explosion of pain hit Hagano's ear as Jaga's staff collided with his head. Everything blurred. A breathy moan escaped his lips as his body toppled to the floor.

"Hagano?" Jaga's voice felt buried under the pain.

"You're not learning." The sylph climbed onto the railing where Hagano had stood just a moment ago. The sylph's blurry image held a foot over the edge before letting himself fall off.

Jaga's strained groans punctuated her crashing onto the stone floor. She and the sylph had switched again—leaving Jaga to take the fall.

The sylph swung his foot into Hagano's ribs. The blunt force expelled air from his lungs.

Hagano gasped for breath. The heat of the fire stung his eyes, but his vision sharpened. A wall of flame stretched out in front of him. Somewhere in it sat Capheo's book. *Go get it.* He coughed. *Stupid. It's gone. You failed.*

"Tell me." The cockiness in the sylph's voice came to the forefront. "What exactly are you two doing here? Shouldn't you be at home, trembling at the thought of The Sylph King?"

Jaga and the sylph circled each other.

She brandished her staff. "I'm not much one for trembling in fear."

"It's no use, Jaga." Hagano sat up. "He's got a power, like the seven saints. He can switch places with someone... somehow."

"I know." Jaga stopped pacing as she reached Hagano's side. "But I'm not without a few tricks myself."

Something about the threat made the sylph flinch. He pulled out his rapier. "Oh? Do tell. I could always use a little more fun."

"It wouldn't be much of a trick if I explained it beforehand." She stepped closer to the sylph.

He stepped back.

She took another step forward. "Don't tell me you're feeling shy."

"Hardly. Now let us begin, in three..." The sylph held up three fingers. "Two." He lowered a finger and walked to the railing.

"This again?" Jaga flung her staff into a latch on her back.

The sylph lowered another finger. "One." He threw himself over the edge.

Jaga flung herself off the second floor. She must have anticipated a switch.

Buzz. The room shifted in an instant. A sinking feeling took hold of Hagano's gut. He was falling. The raccoon-faced man laid on the floor of the second story.

A pair of arms wrapped around Hagano—Jaga's. They collided in the air. Her momentum sent them into a spin. His legs hit the ground first, but the two rolled over each other more times than he could count. The impact jolted his knee, his hip, then his bad shoulder. He screamed. The crushing pain felt as sharp as the day he'd been injured.

The two separated. Jaga rolled again, stopping a few feet away. "You okay?"

Hagano doubled over. His good hand hovered over his throbbing shoulder. He bit his tongue and fought back a wail.

Buzz. He was back on his feet on the second level. His legs trembled. Collapsing to the floor, he tried grabbing the railing, but missed. His whole body shook. The throbbing in his shoulder pulsed up his neck and down his arm. His head felt light—either from the pain or the switching, he couldn't tell.

Footsteps and grunts sounded from the first level.

The heat from the burning library dried out his eyes. He closed them. *You failed.* To his right burned the book Ecret meant for him to find. Down below, Jaga fought against a sylph neither of them had much hope in defeating. *You're useless. Again.* The fears and doubts that haunted him about his failed guard training returned.

The pulsing pains ebbed into an ache.

He sat up. *Don't!* His mind clicked. Something in the back of his mind told him to lay flat. He laid back down.

Everything is a puzzle, young Hagano. Ecret's words returned to him. *A box. A conversation.* The voice in Hagano's head turned into his own. *A fight?*

A wave of hope lit up inside him. Maybe they did have a chance at defeating the sylph. He had only to solve the puzzle. Jaga was a piece. The sylph was a piece. And so was Hagano.

Each time the sylph switched places with him, he found himself looking at where he had just been. Perhaps the power required the sylph to be looking at his target. That's why something told Hagano to stay low to the ground—to stay out of sight. If the sylph couldn't see him, then they wouldn't switch places. Hagano chewed on his lip. The sylph seemed to like switching with someone on the floor above him, then jumping off. He could keep doing that to Jaga and Hagano over and over, back and forth, so long as the sylph had both of them to switch with. If Jaga were alone, she could jump down and keep him from pulling that same trick.

A lump hit Hagano's throat. He was the weak link. He didn't know how to jump down a level and not injure himself, but Jaga did. He'd have to sneak down to the first floor without being seen, otherwise he and Jaga would keep getting hurt. He pushed himself onto his knees and crawled.

"Who do you serve?" Jaga's voice cut through the air.

The sylph laughed. "What a boring question."

A crash of clanging metal echoed through the chamber.

Now past the library entrance, the aches in Hagano's shoulder faded to a dull soreness. He got on his feet and hunched over, letting him travel faster but still out of sight. The minutes it took to sneak to the stairs felt like hours. His palms sweat. His heart raced.

The cool air of the stairwell filled his lungs with relief. He made it. No more forced falling. Creeping down the stairs, he hid behind a corner to remain unseen. He took in a deep breath and peeked into the chamber of the seven saints.

Artifacts rested on display throughout the room—armor, books, weapons, clothes. Jaga and the sylph stood opposite each other, panting heavily. She held out her staff. He extended his rapier.

She lunged. They switched places. His rapier flew straight into her chest.

"Noo!" Hagano ran into the room.

Unfazed, Jaga wrapped her arms around the sylph's neck and squeezed.

Buzz. A choking grip strangled Hagano for only a second. But he was looking at the sylph, almost confirming that a switch required the proper eyeline.

Jaga released her stranglehold. "Hagano."

Hagano held his hand to his throat and glanced at Jaga. "You're alive? How?"

"I told you, I have my tricks." Jaga stepped back.

The sylph rolled his eyes. "No need to be cryptic." He held up the hilt of his rapier, the blade gone. "As suspected, she can turn metal into water."

Jaga tensed.

"You have a power?" Hagano swallowed hard. Ecret must have given it to her during the attack.

"Yes." She played with her jaw. "Now get out of sight."

"I can help." Hagano straightened his posture.

"No, Hagano. Unlike most enemies, strength in numbers won't work on him. This fight can only be done one on one." She cracked her knuckles.

A sense of guilt arrested him. *Useless. Again.* No. If he couldn't fight physically, he'd fight with his intellect. "I believe his power requires him to be looking at you. I will try to help from the shadows."

She nodded.

Hagano backed away, unsure if the sylph would let him go. To his surprise, he managed to duck out of sight behind a display case.

"Just me and you now." The sylph held his hands together and bowed his head. "The name is Lowell." He stretched out a hand toward Jaga, waiting for her own introduction.

A moment of silence passed. Jaga offered nothing but an indifferent look.

"And you are?"

"In a hurry," Jaga said.

Hagano's mind strained for a strategy that would defeat Lowell. He shook his head. Hand to hand seemed fruitless. She would have to be able to strike Lowell without him seeing. Jaga had already tried choking the sylph from behind. That failed, thanks to Hagano. If they could somehow blind the sylph, his power would be gone. But there was far too much light next to the burning library.

"Fine then." Lowell sighed. He stood up straight, took a deep breath and ran towards Jaga.

She blocked and dodged every punch and kick. Her switch to the defensive would help keep her alive, but would not lead to victory.

Hagano focused on every movement. One lesson from training leapt to the front of his mind. Alessi made sure all trainees understood one basic principle—the enemy will never tell you his weakness, but he will show it to you. Every punch, every strike, every moment was a chance to uncover an enemy's vulnerability.

Lowell attacked over and over to no avail until finally he left Jaga an opening.

She thrust her fist towards his face.

Buzz. They switched places. His fist stopped short in front of Jaga's forehead. She hadn't put enough force into the punch to actually land it. Jaga lifted a knee to strike, but they switched again. His knee hit her ribs. She stumbled backwards.

Lowell chuckled. "Clever. Almost."

Jaga had anticipated the switch, letting her throw a punch without intending to make contact. For the briefest of seconds, she got one step ahead and created an opening—but it failed.

Hagano clenched his teeth. It seemed anticipating a switch wouldn't be a path to victory. Switching happened too fast and could be done back-to-back, making the fight practically symmetrical. It's like fighting yourself. He'd have to think of a way to break the symmetry.

Lowell sat on a nearby table, keeping his distance from Jaga. She burst into a sprint and took hold of a sword on display.

Hagano silently cheered. This was exactly what they needed—a weapon that could only hurt Lowell. But could Lowell switch places and take the sword in her hand or would the weapon stay with Jaga when they switched? Hagano squeezed his eyes closed as he thought back. The book—when he first switched stayed with him. Their clothes didn't switch each time either. And when he threw the book over the balcony to Jaga, Lowell switched before she caught it. Maybe that meant if he waited until the book was in her arms, he couldn't have stolen it.

Jaga inched toward the sylph like a stalking tiger.

Lowell held out his hand. "Have you ever seen chimpanzees in the wild?"

Jaga paused for a moment before landing close enough to strike. The lull in fighting gave them each a moment to catch their breath. "No."

Lowell scrunched his face. "Funny how someone so apish knows so little about chimps." The sylph sat up, losing a bit of casualness but still acting at ease. "I suppose you might not have them in this country. Shame. They're fascinating. Did you know that chimps—"

Jaga swiped the blade at Lowell, but the two traded positions.

"...will wage war," continued Lowell without missing a beat.

Yes! Hagano tightened his fists. The sword was still in Jaga's hand. One more piece of the puzzle locked into place. Click.

"A group of male chimps will gather and infiltrate another tribe's territory." Lowell backed away and sat down in a nearby chair.

His refusal to turn his back on Jaga all but confirmed Hagano's suspicion that his power did, in fact, rely on sight.

"They'll walk around very nervously, startling at every noise, searching the treetops for any sign of enemies. I can't say I know what a chimpanzee thinks, but I do know that walking into someone else's territory does give you a fear of being ambushed." Lowell licked his lips. "And if those chimps are ambushed by a force greater than themselves, they'll flee. If, however—"

Jaga stood up from the table Lowell had placed her on.

"Ah. Ah. Ah." Lowell switched the two of them again, sitting Jaga in the chair and putting himself back down on the table. "We're talking."

She paused before settling into the seat. It seemed she and Hagano had no choice but to listen to Lowell's ramblings. It felt like stalling, but his gut disagreed. There was something to this story that Hagano couldn't put his finger on. Something didn't add up. *Is he waiting for reinforcements?* Looking through the great chamber, Hagano didn't see anyone.

"If the group of young, male chimps run across a stray chimp from another tribe who is out on his own, minding his own business, they'll attack. They pin him, if it's a him, to the ground and bite and beat the life out of him. It's not quick either. He suffers." Lowell looked at the display case that obscured Hagano.

He ducked back behind it, stricken by the fear that he would be seen and thrust back into battle. Nothing happened.

"And if it's a female, they might let her go. Most interestingly, if she's carrying a child, they will snatch up her young and devour it. Strange, don't you think? Chimpanzees do not eat a lot of meat. But in this circumstance, they turn to cannibalism." Lowell paused to look at Jaga as if expecting her to find the same fascination in his story as he did. "But why do they do this? Why venture out of the safety of one's own land? For territory? Is it just their nature? Is it just for fun? How would anybody ever know?"

"What point are you trying to make?" Jaga rubbed her temple.

"So blind. All of you." Lowell licked his teeth. "You cannot see what is right in front of you." He smiled in a way that bordered menacing and sincere. He cleared his throat. "Let's get this over with." He jumped off the table and charged.

She shot out of the chair and swiped at Lowell with the sword.

They switched places.

She stumbled as she continued Lowell's dash. She swung the sword again.

They switched.

Her movements faltered, held back by what appeared to be hesitation.

Hagano's gut churned. He hadn't yet figured out how to solve the puzzle and Jaga needed help.

The sword flew once more.

They switched.

The constant swapping made Hagano dizzy.

Jaga swung again.

They switched.

Think. Think. Think. Think. Think.

It seemed Lowell's only counter to the sword was to switch places.

Jaga stood still.

Hagano wasn't sure what she was planning, but a calm look crossed her face. The arc of her lips hinted at a newfound confidence. *Did she learn something? Something that could make a difference?* He hadn't spotted anything.

Jaga lifted the sword up to her side and swung as if to cut through Lowell's neck.

They switched.

Now in Lowell's place, she lifted her arm in the same manner and made an identical swing.

They switched again.

Lowell hadn't changed the course of Jaga's first swing—he still had a sword moving toward his throat.

He switched them again.

The second motion Jaga started continued. The sword pushed

closer to Lowell. Even if he switched again, he would wind up in the same problem. They were both making the same motion.

They switched, then switched, then switched over and over until the two bodies blurred together into a nonsensical one. The air around them buzzed.

The switching halted.

Both Lowell and Jaga collapsed. She turned her head to vomit, barely able to hold herself up. The sword clanged as it fell to her side. Lowell too struggled on the ground.

"I do not like doing that." Lowell fought to rise from the ground as he lifted himself onto his feet. "You..." He gasped for air. "Are a lot more fun than..." He wheezed. "Anyone else I've killed." He panted for a beat before his breath began to level out. "Except maybe your stupid chicken god."

"Lowell!" shouted Hagano from behind the case. Jaga trembled on the floor from the switching blitz. Hagano needed to buy her some time. She wasn't recovering as fast as the sylph. "I like your weird face ink. You look like a raccoon, but a good-looking one."

Silence.

Hagano had used this tactic many times against Alessi. If they were arguing, Hagano would start complimenting his brother, which would only agitate and confuse him. "I think I might get the same thing on my face. Do you think it would look good on me?"

Lowell huffed. "Mock all you want. You'll be dead in moments."

"I'm not mocking you." Hagano crawled to the other end of the case and peeked out at Lowell. The sylph had turned his attention to where Hagano was hiding, but it looked like the sylph hadn't pinpointed Hagano's location. "Really, I'm not. I like it. I want to do it too. Where did you get yours done?"

"The markings are spiritual. Nothing you would understand."

Hagano tilted his head. Sylphs weren't spiritual creatures. They were slaves. No, worse. They were dirt—the literal landscape of hell upon which The Sylph King trod.

Jaga quivered.

"Uh... and your name. What a name. Looll?" Hagano ducked

back behind the case. Upsetting Lowell might buy some time, but he also didn't want to be thrown back into the fight.

"It's *Lowell*," said the sylph, pouring on an even thicker accent. "As in 'wolf pup'."

"Okay, yeah," Hagano shouted. "That's admittedly pretty great. But then why raccoon markings?"

Hagano peeked out just in time to see Jaga find her footing again. His rambling had worked. *Who would have thought my greatest weapon was being annoying?*

Jaga rushed to Lowell, slightly crouched, and thrust her fist up towards his chin.

They switched.

Lowell's fist punched the air above Jaga's head. His eyes stared up at the ceiling.

Jaga crouched below his field of vision and punched upwards a second time. Her knuckles hit his jaw.

Lowell rolled backward.

Jaga threw her elbow into his stomach. She'd broken the symmetry using the difference in height.

A mix of pride and shame struck Hagano. Jaga had turned the tide of the battle, but Hagano wasn't the one who saw the flaw in Lowell's power. *How did I not see it?* It felt so simple—Jaga's shorter stature made the fight asymmetrical.

A thought tugged on Hagano's mind. Jaga didn't need to break the symmetry—she needed to utilize it. "Jaga!" Hagano peeked out from the case. "Don't fight against his power. Combine it with yours."

Jaga trudged back to the sword and picked it up.

Lowell spat out a mouthful of blood. "This again?" He propped himself against the wall and motioned at the sword.

Jaga approached, stopping just a few paces in front of him.

Once again, she swung the sword.

They switched.

Holding the sword in front of her, she spun the blade around. In one swift movement, she plunged the blade into the wall by her side, fixing it in place. She swept a finger across its middle, using her power to melt a sliver of the sword into water and splitting the blade in two. A giant needle protruded from the wall as if someone had stabbed a sword through it from the other side.

"Curious little ideas you seem to be having." Lowell wiped his wrist across his bleeding lip.

She thrust the sword at Lowell's heart, but the two switched places. Jaga turned the blade back at her and crouched. She plunged the short sword into the ground and melted off the handle, creating a second needle that stood diagonally, pointing at Lowell. Jaga stepped in front of the sword shard. Jumping, she kicked Lowell toward the blade that protruded from the wall.

She started to fall towards the needle in the ground. Her aim was perfect. They were both aligned just right that the needles would pierce each of their backs.

A look of dread washed over Lowell's face. The two switched back and forth, but neither position would save him. The broken blade cut into his back from the floor. He switched with Jaga again. The needle from the floor stayed in his back. The needle in the wall cut into him.

Jaga landed. A small puddle watered the floor around her.

Lowell hung from the blade in the wall, gushing blood.

Jaga rose from the ground. She sighed heavily, her shoulders hunched over, and approached Lowell.

The sylph coughed. He muttered something in a foreign tongue as his voice trailed off. His eyelids fluttered until falling shut. Slumping over, his movements ceased.

An unsettling quiet permeated the room.

"Can I come out now?" called Hagano from the case.

"Yes," said Jaga. She limped towards him.

Hagano drug a chair to her. "Are you okay?" He looked her over, seeing if there was a wound he could tend to, not that he knew how.

"I'm fine." She fell into the chair. Her eyes locked onto Lowell as he fought to hold up his head. "Good thinking back there. Combining the powers and all."

The compliment unknotted Hagano's stomach. "Thank you. I just..." He looked over to Lowell. "Wanted to help." His attention turned to the flames in the library. "I didn't get a chance to read the book though. I have no idea what it was supposed to teach me."

Jaga held her side as she took deeper and deeper breaths. "I assume it would tell you what that key was for." She cleared her throat. "Hopefully one of the other guards found out the key's purpose before the library went up in flames."

The thought soothed him. He'd failed, but maybe all was not lost. "Yes. Hopefully."

Lowell coughed.

Both Hagano and Jaga whipped their heads toward the sylph.

The sylph's head bobbed as he struggled to hold it up.

A buzz irritated Hagano's ears as he found himself leaning against the wall.

Lowell fell over Jaga's lap. "He will kill you for this." The sylph's body went limp and rolled onto the floor. The sword, split in two, stuck out of his robes and shimmered in the light of the fire.

CHAPTER TWELVE

REFLEXES

T he fiery light from the burning library cast moving shadows on the walls of the chamber.

"Is he dead now?" Hagano returned to Jaga's side, but kept an eye on the body face-down in front of her.

Jaga pushed Lowell's shoulder with her foot. "Yes." She glanced around the room until her eyes landed on the hilt of the rapier on the floor. "Thirsty?"

Thirsty? The thought felt dumbfounding. "Yes... I am." Hagano nodded. "How'd you know?"

"You've been smacking your tongue."

He hadn't noticed.

She pointed down at the rapier's hilt. "Pass that to me."

"Sure." Hagano scooped it up and tossed it her way. "How are you doing? Are you hurt?"

"Yes, but nothing serious. I just need to rest for a moment." She knelt on the ground and pushed the hilt against the stub of the blade sticking out of Lowell's back.

"What are you doing?"

"Getting us something to drink." The hilt and the blade fused together. With a sharp jerk, she extracted the broken rapier.

"What kind of something?" Hagano scratched his arm.

The light of the burning library reflected off the sword as she used Lowell's robes to wipe clear his blood.

"Ah." Hagano nodded. If Jaga could turn metal to water, then every piece of metal was also something to drink. "Have you ever used your power to drink water before? I mean, the metal-water... water." The idea of putting a sharp blade in his mouth made him flinch. Thinking about how that blade also killed Lowell made him nauseous.

She gripped a piece of the rapier. It broke off in her hand. "Yes, many times."

Hagano couldn't tell if she was making a joke.

Placing the metal in her mouth, Jaga paused and then gulped loudly. Like breaking a twig, she snapped off another piece and offered it to Hagano. "Here."

"Thanks." He looked at Jaga, almost expecting her to tell him this was a joke. "This isn't gonna cut me, right?" The metal felt cold on his tongue.

"Not if you're careful." Jaga tapped Hagano's lips with a finger.

The metal liquified, filling his mouth with water and soothing his dry throat. He anticipated the sword tasting metallic or odd in some way, but found it surprisingly pure. The drink revived each part of him as if a light spread down his chest, through his arms, and coursed in his veins.

"We should go. Someone might have heard us." Jaga drank more of the rapier. She took a few steps towards an adjacent hall, favoring one leg.

Hagano jogged up to her side. He hunched slightly and motioned to her arm as if to crouch underneath it. "May I?"

"Thank you." Jaga rested some of her weight on him.

"You're welcome." Hagano grinned, hoping he wasn't making her feel pitied. He'd spent months turning down offers for help when dealing with his bad shoulder, even though sometimes he needed it. Pity annoyed him.

"I promise I don't feel as bad as I look." Jaga lost her footing.

Hagano kept her from falling. "Maybe you should sit down for a minute. We can try to plan our next move while you recover."

A curt '*hm*' sounded enough like an agreement for Hagano to keep pressing forward.

"Let's just get somewhere out of sight." The idea of picking her up crossed Hagano's mind, but something told him that Jaga wouldn't go for it.

"You seem quite comfortable helping me walk. I get the feeling you've done this before."

Hagano nodded and readjusted her arm. "Yes. My parents aren't in the best of health, my dad especially. I swear he is never going to die though. He will just keep getting wrinklier and wrinklier until he shrivels into nothing more than a raisin with nose hair."

Jaga started to laugh, but it turned to a cough.

They moved through the corridors until the light of the fire gave way to the darkness of the night.

"Let's stop here." Jaga motioned to the moonlight shining through a small window. She pulled away from Hagano, leaned against the wall and lowered herself to the floor. Her hands went to work tearing her sleeves. "Rip these into strips."

Sitting, Hagano took the fabric and pulled them apart. The moonlight revealed faded scars along Jaga's now bare arms. His eyes lingered on the lines on her skin, forcing him to wonder where they came from. "How did you put the hilt back on the blade?"

"I can turn metal to water *and* water to metal. It took a little back and forth, but I managed." Jaga held what was left of the rapier over her wounds. The metal cascaded over her arm, washing off dirt and blood.

"Ah." Hagano handed the strips of cloth to Jaga. The process by which her power worked still felt beyond explanation. "You seem so accustomed to using your power, especially after having it only a short time."

"Twelve years is hardly short." She tied a strip of cloth around her arm.

"Twelve years?" The question echoed in Hagano's head.

"Give or take." She tied another knot.

"You had a power before the attack?" Hagano's mind blanked trying to make sense of the information. He'd spent his entire life believing Ecret hadn't shared his powers with humans since overthrowing The Sylph King. There was no need. The god's peace went unchallenged for six centuries—until today.

Jaga nodded. "Yes. It's not something the public knows."

"But why?" Something felt wrong. "There's barely any crime in the capitol or the whole country. It seems unnecessary."

Jaga shifted the way she was sitting, leaning more to one side. "Well, there are times when Ecret's empowered saints are given especially difficult tasks—ones that might require a bit more ability. It's not something that concerns most people."

"Well, it seems to concern *most people* now." Hagano frowned. He was eighteen and she was nearing forty, he assumed. They were allies, but her tone made it clear that she didn't see him as a peer.

"I know it must be confusing, but let's focus on the task at hand. We need to keep moving."

Hagano scoffed, but knew she was right. "Is that all you're going to tell me?"

"If you've learned anything today, it should be that there are greater threats out there than pickpockets and thieves. If you don't believe me, go take another look at the dead man back there." She pointed back towards Lowell.

"He's not a man. He's a sylph." Hagano played with his jaw. This conversation felt like he was a three-year-old learning about the basics of life. Don't play by the fire, you could get burned. Don't play by the river, you could drown. Don't believe everything Ecret taught you, it wasn't all true. He huffed. Maybe none of it was true.

"The Sylph King doesn't transfer his powers to his slaves, Hagano. That person back there is just that—a person." Jaga tightened the last bandage around her leg.

"How does that make any sense?"

"No idea." Jaga shrugged. "But he was clearly lying about his master being The Sylph King and it's a little late to interrogate him."

"Eat." The strange voice returned.

Hagano whipped his head to look down the hall, thinking someone was there before realizing it was the same voice as before.

"What is it?" Jaga pushed herself up.

"Eat."

Hagano turned his head again, looking in the opposite direction. "Nothing."

Jaga stepped in front of him. Her eyes pierced his, searching him as if they could read his thoughts. "Do you hear someone?"

"No." The word flew out of his mouth before he even thought about it.

She squinted. "Yes, you do."

"Eat." The voice sounded as if it came from all directions.

"I... I..." His vision blurred.

"Don't ignore it." She took his hand. Her demeanor softened. "Listen to it. It's okay. Just let it in."

A long breath cooled his chest. "What is it?" he whispered.

"Listen to it. It will tell you." She released his hand and stepped back.

His whole body tensed. He clenched his hands into fists.

"Eat."

Closing his eyes, he whispered, "Okay." A burnt taste covered his tongue. It climbed down his throat. His eyes shot open.

The dark halls of the temple were gone, replaced by the light of the noon sun.

Hagano stood at a pond. Trees and shrubbery surrounded him. The sun peeked through the forest canopy, reflecting off the peaceful pond water.

"Ecret," called a child's voice from the woods. "You hiding again?"

He looked down at his hands. In a blink, they became white wings tipped with black feathers.

"I'm not hiding!" Hagano yelled back, not in control of his own actions. His voice wasn't his own. It sounded familiar. Like the voice from the woods, his own had the light tone of a young boy's.

He looked down at his wings. A goldfish flopped around in his grasp. He leaned down and popped it into his mouth. A bitter slime made him gag, but he pressed his lips shut to keep the fish inside. Lifting his chin, he swallowed. *You can do this.* Hagano approached the edge of the pond and looked into the water.

The reflection of a small, younger Ecret peered back at him. He didn't wear his usual mask, showing the entirety of his young, human face. The five black horns atop his head hadn't fully grown in and only barely cut through the top of his cowl. Hagano lifted his foot—no, a talon—and tapped the surface of the water. Ripples spread over the surface. An instant annoyance welled up inside him. He tapped the surface again. More ripples spread, but nothing else happened.

A push from behind knocked Hagano off balance and into the water. He turned around and sat in the muddy pond, covered in weeds. "Not funny, Inturon."

A half-boy, half-beast stood at the water's edge. The top half of his head was covered in fur. Cat-like ears poked out of his head. The bottom half of his face melded into a human jaw and mouth. The boy wore a sleeveless shirt, revealing mammalian arms and paws. He flicked his tail and stuck out his tongue. "Whatcha doing?"

"Go away, Inturon." Hagano brushed wet weeds off his head.

"Dad says you still haven't figured it out." Inturon flicked his tail.

Hagano glared at the beast-boy. "So?"

Inturon stared back. "I'm here to help."

"I don't want your help."

A splash burst up as Inturon jumped into the pond next to Hagano. "It's easy." The young Inturon put his paw into the water. A flurry of goldfish sprang into being and swam in a circle around Inturon's paw. "Just think about the animal that you want to make, channel your intentions, and command your body to make it happen."

Hagano looked away.

"Here." Inturon took hold of Hagano's wing and held it under the water. "You want to make goldfish, right?"

Hagano turned his gaze back to Inturon.

"Think about the fish. Focus on your desire to make it appear. Then tell your body to do it." Inturon flashed a smile.

"How?" Hagano pursed his lips.

"Just say the words," Inturon said as if it were obvious.

"Okay." Hagano thought about the goldfish sitting in his stomach. The desperation to create surged inside him. "Body, make a goldfish."

"Don't just say it." Inturon squeezed Hagano's wing. "*Command* your body to do it."

"Okay." Hagano scrunched his face and breathed out his nose. "Make... a goldfish."

Another goldfish splashed into the water. It swam in place, as if waiting for direction.

Hagano fought back a grin. An unexpected gratitude for Inturon emerged, feeling like the same warmth Alessi's encouragement gave him. "Thanks, Inturon."

Inturon, the pond, and the woods faded away. The darkness of the temple returned. Hagano's wings became hands. A live chicken sat on his palms.

"What... just... happened?" Hagano's eye twitched. "Why am I holding a chicken?"

Jaga tsked. "Huh. I never would have guessed."

"Guessed what?" Bending over, Hagano tossed the chicken. It spun around, staring back at him. The pattern of its feathers caught his eye. If he didn't know better, that chicken was Milena—the same bird he defeathered and ate only hours earlier.

"Your power, Hagano. I would have never thought Ecret would give *that one* to you." Jaga crossed her arms.

His whole body felt heavy. "Power? Ecret didn't give me a power."

"Yes." She rolled her eyes. "He did. I assume during the attack." She straightened her posture. "Did Ecret do something to you during the battle? Like, give you an out-of-body sort of experience?"

The feelings of his vision returned. He could see himself, flying through the air in Ecret's talon. The line between him and the rest of the world softened.

"I get it." She shrugged a shoulder. "You're shocked. But this is a good thing." She poked his chest. "Now you have a real weapon to fight with."

"Weapon?" Hagano dropped the chicken and hugged himself. It flapped to the floor.

Jaga gently held his shoulders. "You can summon your own animals. And command them."

"No, I can't." Dread filled his core. Whatever warmth and hope he felt when Ecret gave a sword to him, this was the opposite. His hands felt heavy. The hairs on the back of his neck stood up.

"Yes, you can." She waved at the chicken standing next to them. "Don't believe me? See for yourself. Tell it to do something."

"Like what?" The sight of the chicken nearly choked him.

"Anything." She waved a finger in a circle. "Tell it to walk around."

"I don't know." Hagano shook his head. This didn't feel real.

"Just try." She placed a hand back on his good shoulder.

"Walk—" The memory of Inturon's words cut him off. He needed to not just say it, but *mean* it. Hagano licked his lips and stared at the chicken. As if he were telling a child to behave, he opened his mouth. "Walk in a circle."

Without hesitation, the chicken strutted in a circle.

A wave of goosebumps washed over him. He shivered. "This can't be real."

"Oh, it is." Jaga stepped back and crossed her arms. "And if you think that's impressive, you're in store for a lot more."

Her words put a knot in Hagano's stomach. "What do you mean? How do you know all this?"

"This power you possess, there's a lot more to it. I've seen it before, during my time as a temple guard." Her eyes scanned the chicken. "You can create a lot more than chickens. Your power lets you create, well, any animal."

A flurry of images flashed in his mind as if flipping through the pages of a book. He pictured herds of elephants, swarms of scorpions, and flocks of eagles all converging on his enemies. Rhinos, tigers, and anacondas all leapt into his head, giving him more and more ideas on how he would help fight The Sylph King. He could use gorillas, bears, wolves, spiders, poisonous insects and flesh-hungry beasts. "I can make anything? Any creature?"

"Yes." Jaga nodded. "Any creature whose flesh you have eaten."

The dreams in Hagano's head crumbled. Although not as grandiose of a picture as before, he still held onto a touch of hope. He had always prided himself on not being a picky eater and the capitol city provided him with a plethora of options, including some unusual choices. He had tried snake, frog, scorpion, crocodile, and a host of other meats. The more he thought about it, the more the idea of fighting with an army of beasts created a new sense of courage in him. For the first time, he would be able to contribute to Ecret's cause.

Jaga tsked. "That is anything you've eaten since Ecret gave you that power."

"You mean..." Hagano's eyes rolled upward as he took in Jaga's words. "...everything I've eaten since this afternoon?" His mind traced back through the day. The only meat he had eaten was... chicken. "That is..." His voice trailed off. "...not great."

The wild ideas of commanding a platoon of beasts were quickly replaced in Hagano's head with an image of him holding Milena in his hands and throwing her at his enemies. She was a ruthless bird, pecking people at every turn—but nothing more than a nuisance. His face flushed. Even with power given to him by a god, he still wasn't useful. He averted his eyes. "So, I can make *one* chicken?"

"If you've eaten chicken, you can create many chickens."

"Oh." A touch of excitement returned to Hagano's voice, but left just as quickly. "Is that really any better?"

She tapped her foot on the ground as if she couldn't hold still. "Not yet it isn't. Your first priority should be eating more useful animals."

"Okay." The knot in Hagano's stomach grew. He wasn't sure where to find anything more than chicken. Rabbit, maybe, but that was stupid.

"But now we have another problem." She walked back and forth, her limp fading. "If you have that power, then The Hallux is dead."

"The Hallux?" Hagano couldn't see whatever connection Jaga

made between Hagano's power and the missing hierophant, The Hallux. As one of Ecret's top counselors, he should have attended the festival, but didn't. Hagano assumed the old man was under the weather, not dead. "Why does this mean he's dead?"

Jaga bobbed her head and waved her hands as if thinking aloud. "The Hallux had your power before you. The only way to lose a power is to die. Then it goes back to Ecret and he can bestow it upon someone else."

"Okay…" Hagano fidgeted. Her pacing unsettled his nerves. "But what does that mean?"

She stopped. "I'm not sure, but if the head of our police force died right before the attack, I doubt it was a coincidence."

An eerie thought sprang up in Hagano's head. "Do you think he was murdered?"

"Possibly." She tilted her head.

Hagano's breathing stopped. The thumping of his heart pounded in his ears. If the Hallux who had this power was still killed all the same, how would it actually help Hagano survive? Surely the old man had more time to learn it and more animals in his arsenal, but they were all for naught. Hagano had nothing more than chickens. He gasped for air. "I can't do this."

"Yes, you can." Jaga's words sharpened, cutting into him. She glared.

"No. I can't." He tried to clear the lump in his throat. "With chickens? Really? How is that supposed to help?"

Jaga cleared her throat and spat on the floor. "Lord Ecret gave you that power. He does not hand out gifts like that by accident."

A chill ran up Hagano's back.

She flashed a cold look. "Don't you have faith in him?"

"Yes." The answer shot out of his mouth before he even thought about it. For his whole life, the answer had always been yes. But now the question sat uncomfortably. *Do I have faith in Ecret?* The answer wasn't as easy as it used to be. Ecret was dead. He was supposed to be immortal, but now his lifeless body hung outside the temple walls.

Yes. I do. I still have faith. Was he holding on to something that was never real? He couldn't tell.

"Ecret believes you can use this power. You should too." Jaga straightened her posture, looking more like a soldier. She balled up a fist and lifted it.

"What are you doing?" Hagano held out a hand, not sure if she was preparing to strike.

"You need to learn this power quickly and I have an idea." Her nostrils flared. "The power is there. It is part of you. You just need to know the feeling of using it. It's like learning to walk as a child. When you were a baby, you had legs, but you didn't know how to use them, until you did. Does that make sense?"

"I think so." Hagano squinted and leaned back. "So how does that help?"

Jaga punched Hagano in the nose. A rush of dull pain put water in his eyes.

"Ow." He stepped back and cupped his hand over his nose. "Why would you do that?"

She threw her fist again. A chicken snapped into being between her fist and Hagano's face.

A burnt taste filled Hagano's mouth. His stomach jerked as if to vomit. The feeling of feathers on his skin covered his hands.

The chicken took the brunt of Jaga's punch. Its soft body collided with Hagano's hand, pushing against his already aching nose. The chicken vanished.

"You did it." Jaga's eyes slanted into a smile. "For at least a second there. I'm not sure where the chicken went."

The pain in Hagano's nose spread across his face. Squinting his eyes, he winced. "Why would you punch me?"

"Reflexes." Jaga shook her hand. "It's like the falling reflex in infants."

"The what now?" Hagano frowned, tapping his nose gently with his fingers.

"If you're holding an infant and lower it to give it the sensation of falling, the baby will extend her arms, then pull them back in."

"So I'm like a baby?" Hagano ignored the sting of the comparison.

"Essentially, yes. Like a falling infant, your body will do things on its own out of instinct. The power is there. The instinct is there. I just prompted the response."

He took a step back. "You're not going to punch me again, are you?"

"No." She crossed her arms. "Whatever feeling the reflex produced, I want you to try and replicate it. Hopefully that will get you started."

"Oookay." Hagano took in a deep breath and stretched his neck to one side. "I'll try." He closed his eyes and smacked his lips, thinking about the burnt taste his power left behind. He imagined feathers brushing his skin. His thoughts kept rotating between a burnt flavor, a caressed hand, a wrenching stomach, and the appearance of a chicken. *Mouth, hand, stomach, chicken, mouth, hand, stomach, chicken.*

Nothing happened.

"It's not working." Hagano scratched his head.

"Keep trying."

"But what I'm trying isn't doing anything. I keep thinking 'Mouth, hand, stomach, chicken'." Hagano threw his hand out in frustration. A live chicken materialized in the air and dropped to the floor. His eyes widened.

"Congratulations. You used your power." Jaga's posture relaxed.

Hagano searched the dark hall, still trying to make sense of everything. "I hate to say it, but the punching worked. I think I might know how to use this power." He looked down at the duplicate version of Milena, which felt odd after having already eaten her.

"Good." Jaga held a hand to her heart. "But keep practicing."

Hagano couldn't help but feel inspired. A couple chickens would do nothing to turn the tides, but Ecret's faith in Hagano didn't seem as unfounded anymore. Like many times before, a peaceful sense of gratitude filled him—for Ecret, for Jaga, for Inturon.

The vision of the young bearcat god hadn't faded like his dreams always did. There was a tangible fondness still there, inside that experience—one that Hagano could only compare to his admiration

ADAM BERG

for Alessi. The time with Inturon felt like a memory—Ecret's memory that somehow Hagano could access. The memory, if it was just that, was clearly ancient. Hagano's only guess was that it was something given to him when Ecret handed off his power—like instructions. His affection for Inturon still lingered.

"So...." Jaga patted the fake Milena. "You can make them. Can you unmake them?" A subtle pride shone through her tone.

"I haven't figured that out yet." Hagano bit his lip.

A thunderous crash erupted from the bowels of the temple. A vibration shook the floor, dislodging dust from the walls.

Jaga peered down the hall toward the noise. "No time to find out. We have to go."

CHAPTER THRITEEN
CHASED OFF

The uneven stones of the temple floors sent jolts through Hagano as he ran behind Jaga. Pattering chicken feet followed.

The earth rattled at the sound of another thunderous crash.

Hagano's mind jumped to Alessi, hoping that his brother was safe. Months of lingering resentment vanished. His shoulder stung with every step and labored breath, but the anger in his heart gave way to the fear of losing his brother.

The Sylph King's words returned to him. *Show me the endling.* The endling—the last god, Inturon—Ecret's brother.

Ecret must have refused to surrender his brother during the attack. It cost him his life. After peeking into Ecret's memory, Hagano could feel for himself what it was like to have a younger sibling. He could only imagine Alessi felt the same way about Hagano. As far as he knew, Alessi had sacrificed himself in the same manner when he lured a sylph away from a hiding Hagano.

The hallway opened up into the throne room. Hagano drew his sword.

Another quake erupted.

The sounds could only mean one thing—battle. A fear welled up inside—was he moments away from facing The Sylph King and all he had was a scimitar and some chickens? Failure and eternal suffering seemed inevitable.

Another explosion rang out.

Guards shouted orders to coordinate attacks. Other voices yelled in a foreign tongue—a sign that more than one enemy awaited him. If all of them were as difficult to kill as Lowell and his switching power, no amount of steel would matter.

Dust filled the air of the throne room. Debris lay scattered in every direction. A swarm of stone spiders crawled like ripples in a pond, following the hand motions of a guard standing at the far end of the room. Hagano had seen this power once before. Ecret had used it at the attack. It seemed the god gave out more than one power at the festival.

A platoon of sylphs cut through the oncoming swarm.

Hagano searched every corner for any sign of The Sylph King, but failed to locate him. With any luck, the monster was elsewhere.

Jaga sped toward the guard commanding the stone creatures. Hagano and his chicken followed.

Tendrils of black tar circled a woman at the entrance—the chee-tah-faced warrior that killed the hierophants. The tar whipped the ground, cutting through everything in its path. A man stepped up behind her, his cold demeanor unfazed by the fight in front of him. More markings covered his face, but Hagano couldn't distinguish the pattern through the haze.

Stomping footsteps from behind neared him. Hagano looked back, but saw no one. Something dull smacked his shin as he ran, sending him into a series of flailing steps. He spun around and reached out for balance. Panting, he steadied himself, but couldn't see Jaga.

"Jaga!" He looked around, unsure of how he lost her in so short a moment.

A pair of hands flipped him to the ground. He rolled and looked up at the face of a man with markings on his face—dark circles around his eyes with another patch extending from the point of his nose to his lips—like a lemur. His eyes looked like marbles—one purely white, the other entirely black. Their stare pierced Hagano.

A coldness seeped into his bones, freezing him in place. Ethereal shapes flashed next to this strange man, forming what looked like people. Ghostly hands latched onto Hagano—their touch light, but collectively strong.

The world went silent. Every ounce of him felt heavy. His tongue swelled. Despite all his effort to follow Ecret's teachings and be a good person, this was the end—a path leading straight into the clutches of The Sylph King. He'd die. It didn't matter that he tried to find Ecret's book and threw himself into battle. Ecret wouldn't save him. Ecret *couldn't* save him. And Hagano was useless—like a child or an injured trainee or a simple chicken.

The soft, cold grip of a thousand hands spread over his arms, his legs, and his neck. The will to resist escaped him. The black and white stare of his enemy pinned him.

Help... He blinked.

The chicken flapped wildly at the man's feet, pecking over and over. He kicked at it, but the creature dodged left and right. The bird froze. Images of people holding the chicken in place flashed, disappearing and reappearing back and forth. The lemur-faced man stomped, sending the bird out of existence in a swirl of flesh like water draining from a bottle.

Out of the dust, a foot flew through the air, knocking the man over.

Whatever spell the man's ghosts put over Hagano dissipated as the man recovered from the blow. Sounds of the battle returned to Hagano's ears. His heart pumped more adrenaline into his veins.

Alessi appeared at Hagano's side.

"Are you okay?" Alessi kept his eyes on the enemy.

"Alessi, you're alive." The warmth of his brother's presence flooded Hagano as if seeing Alessi had undone the horrors around them.

Alessi stepped between Hagano and the lemur-faced man. He looked over his shoulder. "Glad to see you too."

"I can make chickens." Hagano pushed himself up.

"What?"

Hagano grunted. He wanted to explain what had happened, but his thoughts couldn't put themselves in the right order. "Ecret gave me a power."

"To make chickens?" Alessi flashed a confused look.

"It's better than it sounds." Hagano rolled his eyes. It sounded crazy, but he'd already done it twice. "I'll be able to make other things too, soon."

"Okay."

Their enemy stepped forward. Alessi stepped left to counter.

"Listen." Alessi leaned toward Hagano. "Go to the entrance and help Jaga retrieve Ecret's body."

"What? Why?" Hagano's hand drifted toward the hilt of his sword. He didn't want to leave Alessi again.

"Did you not find your book?" Adjusting his stance, Alessi poised himself to strike.

"I failed." Hagano's heart sank. The all-too-familiar sense of disappointing Alessi found him.

"We're bringing him back." Alessi twitched. "Now go. Help Jaga."

Back? A flurry of questions fought for his attention, but surrendered to a newfound hope. His god could return. The wrongs of the world could be righted. What little faith remained no longer felt foolish. A path to paradise was still possible.

The lemur-faced man clasped his hands together, looking calm. A battalion of ghostly soldiers flickered around him.

Alessi held out his sword. "Now go."

"I'll be back for you." Hagano dashed towards the main gates. He shouted for Jaga until he caught sight of her running outside. The cheetah-woman had cleared the doorway, fighting a group of guards near the guard station. Weaving around rubble and flurries of stone insects, Hagano darted outside.

Ecret's body hung upside down, nailed to the building by its talons.

"Jaga!" He caught sight of her scaling the temple wall. With her power to liquify metal, she'd remove the nail and release Ecret with little effort.

Out of the shadows leapt another woman. She climbed the wall with the ease of a spider. Her joints popped and jutted out like a monster. She rushed to Ecret's feet, reaching it far sooner than Jaga.

He couldn't think of what else to do but yell. "Look out!"

The woman clung to the wall above Jaga, kicking down at her. Jaga caught the woman's foot and jerked it as hard as she could. The woman lost her grip and plummeted to the ground. She crashed hard on her side and laid motionless, black tar oozing out of a hidden wound.

Jaga kept climbing.

Still far from the nail, two more figures jumped onto the building with an inhuman power. One pounced on Jaga, pushing her off the building. Hagano reached out, creating a flock of chickens to soften her landing. The impact unraveled the birds in a blink.

One of the men hopped to the ground and straddled her. He clasped her throat.

She bucked, shoving his arms and undoing their grip. She spun on the ground, wrapped her legs around his arm, and broke his elbow.

The other man leapt to the ground.

Jaga rolled away from him and into a defensive position. They exchanged glances. Hagano's heart raced, not sure how to help her and fearing that once again he might be in her way—like he was with Lowell.

Seconds passed like hours. The two men bounded for her. She ran off, the men on her tail.

An otherworldly crunching and clicking sounded behind him. He turned to see the sylph-woman standing in the puddle of black blood she had spilt. The sanguine mud crawled back to her body and into her pores. Her shoulder snapped back into place. She rotated the joint as if feeling it for the first time. Hagano could see through a hole in her clothes that the tar restored the woman's skin as if it stitched her together seamlessly. She stretched her neck and pushed her ribs back into place. Her head tilted with a snap, her eyes locking on Hagano. She jumped into a sprint.

Hagano fled. Years of sprinting through a crowded city gave him advantage over most people, but what pursued him was no longer a person. Whatever force gave her life also afforded her an agility greater than any man's. But he had to try and outrun her, or at least outmaneuver her in the streets until somewhere safe presented itself.

He panted heavily, refusing to let his shortness of breath slow him down. He made it through the courtyard and into the streets before the woman pounced. He dropped to the ground. She flew overhead. He caught himself with his hand, but his mouth hit the cobblestone. A brief swipe of the tongue and Hagano could feel a chip in his tooth. Blood gushed from his mouth.

A flock of chickens rushed his enemy and sent her into a fluster. Scrambling, he raced down an adjacent street. He could hear clucking and flapping behind him but dared not look back to see how close his enemy was.

Corner after corner he turned until stumbling upon an abandoned shop with an open window. Clambering inside, he pressed up against the wall. His labored breaths drowned out the sounds outside. He gripped his shaking sword in terror. Either he would be found and would have to fight or he'd spend his time suffering the torture of waiting. Adrenaline surged through him so rapidly he felt his heart might explode. His fear painted a picture in his mind of the woman standing just outside the shop, licking her lips like a hungry predator.

She had every advantage. She was stronger, faster, and as far as he could tell, incapable of dying.

Panic surged. *Stay calm. Think. It's a puzzle, right? Everything's a puzzle.*

Click—the spark of an idea ignited. His chickens would follow orders and he could make more than one. How many, he wasn't sure, but the more, the better. If all went well, he could organize them into a warning system. He'd just have to tell them to spread out and make noise if they saw her.

With a few quick breaths, Hagano mustered enough courage to peek out the window. An empty alley greeted him. He hopped out of the shop and knelt on the ground. By his command, dozens of birds burst to life—as many as Hagano could summon. More and more filled the alley. Part of him wanted to count, but he held back to not waste time. With a mere thought, the chickens spread out in every direction. If his hunch was right, the chickens would station themselves on every street, in every alley, at every intersection. Then, if one saw her, it would squawk.

The birds followed his orders and spread out. Hagano clutched his sword and crept through the streets. A soft breeze brushed his face and cooled his sweating brow. The cool night felt unnaturally still. His shoulders tensed—his injured one aching. At any second, a bird would see her and sound. Then he could tell them to swarm her until he had a chance to land a fatal blow—somehow.

A pebble fell at his side.

Hagano looked up. His eyes found the woman standing on the roof above him. She hopped off the building, snapping both her legs. Bone jetted out from her skin, followed by spurts of tar. The chickens flocked her in a frenzy. She batted them away as her legs reconstructed themselves.

Hagano charged. If victory were possible, it would have to be now.

Flapping and clucking, the chickens vanished one by one before being replaced by a new wave.

Hagano flicked his blade, slicing through both a chicken and the woman's throat.

She flinched.

The tip of the sword sizzled away as her blood corroded it.

Hagano swallowed hard. If his sword decreased with every swipe, his attacks were numbered. He needed to decide the fight as quickly as possible. Only one theory sprang to mind, thanks to Alessi. If it didn't work, he'd have to run again.

The woman's throat and legs repaired themselves.

Hagano clenched his jaw and created a chicken in the air above the woman.

She swatted it, giving Hagano an opening to drive his sword into her chest and through her heart. With all his strength, he plunged the blade, pushing her against the wall.

Her arms dropped and swayed at her side. She hunched over as the force keeping her alive abandoned her. Hagano watched intently, not ready to believe that he had won. If her blood is what gave her power, then destroying her heart might cut her off from that power. That is, after all, how Alessi had killed one of these monsters during the festival attack.

Blood spewed out of her wound.

Hagano took in a deep breath. The tension in his muscles eased. Relief swelled, dispelling the oppressive fear that covered every inch of him.

The woman grabbed his arms. She dug her nails into his skin, drawing blood. Her fingers cut like daggers.

He screamed and pulled in vain against her grip. His weak shoulder gave out, popping in an explosion of pain as his arm slipped from its sling. *Why aren't you dead?!*

The woman pulled his hands off the sword and towards her bleeding chest.

Hagano's shoulder cracked, multiplying the pain. Over and over, he tried to jerk free but to no avail. Flinging himself left and right offered no relief. His efforts only made her nails dig deeper.

She pressed Hagano's hands into her wound, covering them with the caustic tar.

A primeval cry escaped his lips. Pain, greater than any he'd ever imagined, blinded him. This wasn't happening—right? It couldn't be.

The tar ate through his skin, his muscles, his bones. The woman clenched tighter, pulling his hands into her wound. Hagano's fingers dissolved, then his palms and his wrists. He wailed in agony, his lungs heaving. Tears poured down his cheeks. He tried to will the birds to his aid, but none came.

Inch by inch, the woman pulled his arms into her blood, dissolving his forearms. She dragged his arms into the black ichor until her hands too started to dissolve in the acid. Bit by bit, her hands and his arms disintegrated until she didn't have enough of a hand to hold Hagano in place.

He flung himself onto his back.

Void of life, she too collapsed to the ground.

Weeping and shrieking, Hagano flailed. His screams echoed through the alleys around him. *This isn't real! It isn't real! Please....* He held out what remained of his arms. His elbows melted into nothing more than searing pain and toxic fumes.

CHAPTER FOURTEEN

DELIRIUM

Hagano's head spun. He shivered with pain. Tears welled in his eyes, blurring the sky as he looked up into it. A pool of blood chilled his back, sticking his clothes to his skin.

Shades of orange washed away the grey of night. What little warmth the morning sun offered did nothing to alleviate Hagano's suffering. His eyelids fluttered. Air struggled to reach his lungs, catching in his throat as an achy croak. *Make it stop. Just make it stop. Please. It hurts.*

A foggy spell clouded his mind. The last of his strength waned. His eyes closed for what he knew would be the last time. A breeze caressed his ear.

A sea of white sand filled the darkness around him. The pain dulled. He was back on his feet. *Is this death?* He looked down at his arms. Muscles and bone ended at the elbow. Black sludge coated the stubs. He gasped for breath. The chalky taste of the air made him cough.

Blood and sludge dripped from what remained of his arms.

Nothing but sand dunes surrounded him. A cloudless grey sky washed out the sun.

He hobbled forward. "Hello?"

Something muffled the sound of his voice. He could barely hear it.

"Hello?" Hagano reached for his ear, forgetting for a moment that he had no hands. Swallowing, he popped his ears to try and clear whatever it was that kept him from hearing. "Ecret?"

Still muffled.

"Alessi?" The word sounded like he was underwater. The thought of his brother stung. They'd never see each other again—not if The Sylph King had any say.

Hagano looked behind him, hoping to see someone that could help. Nothing. He turned, searching the horizon for anything other than dunes. Nothing.

"Help!" He tried to yell, but his voice didn't carry.

The wind died down, settling into complete silence.

Marching like a drunkard, every footstep felt clumsy and heavy. His back ached. More blood dripped from the exposed muscles in his arms. "Ecret?"

Nothing.

Without any destination in mind, he pressed forward.

Dune after dune passed with no sign of life. No trees. No plants. No Ecret. The only thing that changed was him getting more and more light-headed.

Hagano reached the top of another dune. At long last, something caught his eye. In the distance, the sand dropped off at a cliff. Something to go toward.

The emptiness of death left him numb. Ecret wasn't here to ferry him to paradise, but neither was The Sylph King. He didn't feel hope, but despair had yet to reach him. He moaned, trying to breathe. The stories of sylphs piled on top of each other, paralyzed and suffering didn't match the barren landscape before him. At least, not yet.

Hours seemed to pass before Hagano neared the cliff's edge. All sense of time abandoned him. Every moment stretched into days. He shambled forward. His head dizzied. Drip by drip, his blood dotted the sand. The cliff's edge neared.

Below the rocky crest, countless people filled the expanse of a massive chasm. Most were broken in pieces, maimed, injured, and bleeding. Some of them moaned, but their collective voices barely reached Hagano's ears.

His mind blanked. His knees shook. His heart raced. *It happened. I'm dead. I'm damned. It's over. I will never reach paradise.* His stomach wrenched.

The faintest clunk, like the drop of a pebble, echoed behind Hagano. He turned around. A figure stood in front of him. Hagano wheezed a breathless scream and stumbled backwards.

The Sylph King towered over him. The monstrous demon stood as tall as Ecret, a shadowy cloak masking his body. Bones jutted out of him at seemingly random points. Dozens of rusted swords protruded from his back, a testament to the countless people who'd failed to assassinate him.

Hagano tripped over himself, nearly falling into the chasm. A thousand stories of The Sylph King crashed into his thoughts.

The Sylph King's victims suffered endlessly, buried in a mound of the damned—unable to move, to eat, to talk.

Thousands of generations ago, the gods united to kill the shadowy tyrant. But none could kill what was already dead. So they trapped him inside the mountain barrier. Ecret stayed inside the barrier, with a band of seven saints, to banish the sylphs and keep them from escaping to the rest of the world.

Ecret promised to ferry worthy souls to paradise where The Sylph King had no power. But the promise meant nothing if Ecret couldn't keep it.

The Sylph King stomped a foot on Hagano's chest, pinning him to the ground. "You need to stop the bleeding."

A breeze blew sand into Hagano's eyes.

He blinked over and over until his vision cleared. He looked back up to The Sylph King, but the demon was gone. In his place stood the last person he expected—Ecret.

"Lord?" Hagano fought back tears. "You're here."

"You're going to bleed out and die." The god's voice lacked its usual warmth.

"But I'm already dead."

"Not yet." Ecret's talon wrapped around Hagano and pulled him to his feet.

"I'm not?" Hagano looked down on himself, then back to his god. "Does that mean you're not dead either?"

"No." Ecret tilted his head. "It is of the utmost importance that you understand that I am indeed dead."

"I don't understand." Hagano slouched, his strength fading.

The god's eyes flashed orange. "Death is the separation of body and spirit. The spirit moves on. The body wastes away. Your spirit is still connected to your body."

Hagano nodded. "But your body...."

"My spirit's connection has been severed. My body proper now hangs outside the temple walls. However, I have created a space inside the temple to temporarily anchor my spirit to this world. I cannot go outside the temple walls, but there is a way to restore me." The orange light of Ecret's eyes brightened.

The barren sandscape swirled into a new shape, mimicking the entrance to the temple. Hagano and Ecret looked up at Ecret's lifeless body dangling from above the gate.

"You must return my body to the interior of the temple." Ecret brushed his wing over the corpse's chest. "Once inside, my spirit will be able to rejoin it."

"That's it?" Hagano furrowed his brow.

"There's more." Ecret led Hagano through the temple doors and into the throne room. The cheetah-faced woman stood there. "You must kill this woman. She has taken my blood and mixed it into her tar. Without it, I cannot return to life."

"How could I possibly kill her? She's the one who killed *you*."

Ecret raised a talon and reached for Hagano's face.

He leaned away.

"Dear boy." The god's voice warmed Hagano's heart. "I have trans-ferred a portion of my power to you."

"Yes. I know." Hagano nodded, still unsure how the power to

make chickens could reclaim Ecret's blood. His eyes glossed over. "Wouldn't it be more useful if you gave me a different power?"

Ecret shook his head. "No. You already have one. A second would overwhelm your mortal frame and kill you. Besides, I cannot transfer power without my body. We will have to make do."

Hagano wanted to grumble, but something about being in Ecret's presence made him mind his manners. "Lord?" A handful of questions had been stewing inside him. "Why did you choose me for this?"

Ecret hummed to himself. "When I saw the puzzle box Alessi gave you, I had an idea. I knew you had a sharp mind and a willingness to serve."

"So you replaced the box with one of your own." Hagano bit his lip.

"Yes." Ecret waved his wing. A puzzle box appeared in the air. "I knew if you could solve the box, you could help restore me."

Hagano stared at his feet. His stomach twisted. "I didn't solve it."

"What do you mean?" The tip of Ecret's wing lifted Hagano's chin.

"I broke it open." Hagano sniffed.

Craning his neck down to look Hagano eye to eye, Ecret's eyes creased in a smile. "Breaking open the puzzle box was the only way to solve it."

Hagano's mouth formed an 'o'.

"I needed someone who could look past their preconceived notions and look at the world in a way he never had."

"Wait." Something clicked inside his head, like a puzzle piece locking in place. "You gave me the box before the attack. You knew it would happen."

Ecret's smile vanished. "Yes."

"So you looked into the future and saw that I would help restore you?" Hagano would have beamed had he the energy.

Shaking his head, Ecret stepped back. "No. Not even the gods can see the future. We don't see it, we don't know it, and we certainly don't control it." He paused. "But we still plant seeds."

The warmth and joy of Ecret's words relaxed Hagano. The dull aches of his arms hardly bothered him as he thought about the faith his god put in him. "I was the seed you planted."

"One of many." Ecret bowed his head.

Hagano nodded. Part of his question felt unanswered. "But why me over...someone else? There must have been better people that could have solved the box and used this power."

Ecret took a deep breath. "Giving you the box was a very deliberate chose. You have a sharp mind. The power, though, was less intentional."

A wave of defeat weighed down Hagano. "What?"

"I couldn't reach many of the guards. Some had died. Some were injured. Some were fleeing. You, however, stood in a rather easily accessible location. You were there and I could reach you."

"It wasn't because you knew I would make a difference." Hagano's stomach sunk to his feet. "I was just... there."

"Yes." Ecret's face looked stern. "Whatever series of events led you to that place, it doesn't matter. What matters is that you have my power. Destined or not, this is your path."

Hagano's eyes widened as he stared at the ground. He'd been chosen... on accident? In one fell swoop, every ounce of faith he'd placed in himself died. He looked up into Ecret's glowing, orange eyes. "I wish you had lied to me."

Ecret tilted his head.

"I was hoping you'd say you chose me because you knew I would succeed." Hagano dropped to his knees.

"Like I said, I don't know the future." Ecret's voice brought warmth. "I understand that my telling you the truth may cause you to lose faith, but hear this. You have potential. You have power. You can succeed, though I am afraid you will soon fail."

The words hit Hagano like a punch to the gut. "That doesn't inspire much confidence."

"It is the truth." The white sands of death replaced the scene of the temple. "Lies and deceit are weapons we use against our enemies, not our friends." Ecret's image began to fade into the air like smoke. "What I mean to say is that you are nearing death."

A lump hit Hagano's throat. "Can you save me?"

"No." Only the glow of Ecret's orange eyes remained. "But you can."

"What do I do?"

The last trace of Ecret disappeared.

"Help me!" Hagano fell to his knees. "What do I do?"

The wind kicked up.

"Ecret?"

"Eat." The unknown voice boomed inside his skull.

CHAPTER FIFTEEN

ALONE

The light of dawn dispelled the blackness behind Hagano's eyes. He clenched his eyelids, blocking out the orange glow. His stomach twisted. A stuttering groan pushed its way out his nose. His feet tingled, asleep. Little strength remained—just enough to keep his heart beating. Sharp stings prickled his elbows. He tried to move a hand, but a bolt of pain shot through his arm like lightning. He winced.

Dry air cooled his gums as a he smacked his tongue. He needed water... and food. No. The bleeding... he needed to stop it. Somehow. A sizzling bile shot up his throat. The taste gagged him. Rolling his head to the side, his stomach churned and his chest tightened. A small trace of bile gushed onto his tongue. He spat it out. The acidic liquid stung in much the same way as the tar on his arms, if the degree of pain were at all comparable.

Tears rolled down his cheeks. Unsteady breaths kept his mind from clearing, depriving it of air. A haze of blackness crept into his vision. *Don't fall asleep.* A rush of adrenaline surged. Opening his mouth, he fought for air until the threat of blacking out disappeared. A tremble rippled over his body.

"Tell me what to do."

The plea meant nothing. Eighteen years of turning to Ecret with every need trained him to pray for help at every turn. But the god himself told Hagano he couldn't help—if the trip to the white sands was real. A nagging doubt told him it wasn't. Ecret died. Their conversation moments ago was nothing more than a nightmare.

The image of the souls in the chasm flashed in his mind. He stared up into the sky to push it out.

Soft, white clouds drifted above as if nothing below mattered. Just like any other day, they blew by.

The urge to pray welled up inside him. The world made sense to him two days ago—but not anymore. He sniffed. Life was easier when he believed Ecret could hear his pleas.

"Eat," echoed the deep voice.

Hagano couldn't tell if it was all in his head or if the sounds bounced off the walls of the streets.

The memory of the goldfish forced its way into his thoughts. An image returned to him— the reflection of a young Ecret looking in the water as he tried to make a fish.

More clouds drifted overhead. His eyes glazed over. The whispering of a breeze as the sun rose sent him into a daze. Part of him wanted to die—to end the pain and avoid the likelihood of failing to restore Ecret. The god told Hagano he had planted many seeds. Someone else could do the work, far better than Hagano could— someone Ecret had chosen on purpose. But for the first time in his life, death was no longer a path to eternal peace. It would only be more suffering. That was his choice—give up and suffer forever or keep trying and probably suffer forever.

He swallowed.

No signs of life offered any hope. No people. No animals. Just... emptiness.

He imagined someone, anyone—an old man, a friendly mother, a troubled kid—happening upon him and taking him somewhere safe. Maybe they had seen Jaga, somehow, after she defeated the two sylphs that chased her off. This person could bring him to Alessi, assuming he was still alive.

A jolt shot up his shoulders from the ends of his arms. The slightest twitch awakened his wounds. He exhaled a pained moan. Blackness crept in on him. *No.* He forced deep breaths.

How am I still alive? He tried to figure out how long he'd been unconscious, but no part of his surroundings offered any clues. All he knew was the sunrise, but on which day, he couldn't guess. Had it been minutes? Hours? Days?

His skin felt cold and sticky. Blood pooled at his lower back. Closing his eyes, a fatigue took hold, forcing him to put his strength into opening his eyelids before sleep turned to death.

Death. For the first time, the thought of death felt real. He mumbled a breathy 'hmm'. Odd, how certain death felt. The certainty took away the sting. He didn't need to fight anymore. He lost. While rest no longer waited on the other side, the ease of giving up felt almost comforting. Ending the fight would offer him at least some relief.

Yes. He would die any minute. He'd lost too much blood and there was nothing to do about it. His muscles relaxed. Memories of his family streamed into his thoughts. He could see himself and Alessi playing guard around the house until one of them inevitably broke something and mom started yelling. His father struggled to keep a stern tone while also not caring much about whatever pot had shattered. Knowing how much his family would hurt put a lump in his throat. But under The Sylph King's reign, their time together would be cut short regardless.

He wished one of them were with him, comforting him in his final moment. His mother would run her fingers through his hair as she softly sang a lullaby. His father would hold his shoulder, in silence, until Hagano could no longer feel his soothing presence. Alessi wouldn't sit still. He wouldn't let his brother lie down and die. Hagano almost chuckled. He couldn't imagine his brother giving up on saving Hagano despite all odds. Another wave of tears trickled down his cheeks.

None of them were here. He'd die in the streets all alone.

"Eat."

His thoughts jumped from home, to the goldfish, to eating dinner with his family before heading out to the guard meeting. Milena... that's when he had eaten her.

He clenched his teeth. A copy of Milena burst into being. She stood atop his chest and looked down at him. The duplicate had Milena's exact coloring. He'd seen her thousands of times... at home. The hint of a smile touched his lips. Milena was home.

The words of his mother echoed around him. *I liked Milena.*

Why?

When a chicken's got grit, that's impressive.

The hen stared into Hagano's eyes.

A strange warmth stirred inside him. Something was telling him to keep fighting. Was it Ecret? His mother? Alessi? No. Something else. A feeling he didn't have a name for. A powerful feeling. A convincing feeling.

"I'm an idiot." He stared back at the fake Milena. The allure of death dissipated. His battle wasn't over. Something inside him knew that.

An ounce of strength found him.

Two options presented themselves—return to the temple or go home. Either way, he needed to stop staring at the clouds, get off his back and move forward.

He couldn't know the status of the battle unless he returned to the temple, but going back empty handed could spell certain death. The chances of Ecret having already been restored seemed slim. If the god had already been brought back, he would have made it known. He possessed the ability to communicate with the whole city at once, speaking to everyone's minds. Hagano hadn't yet heard a message. He may have missed it while unconscious though. His gut told him that wasn't the case. His best course of action was to go home and rally himself.

Hagano tightened his core and rolled up his back, trembling as he sat up. Blood dripped from the stubs of his arms as he gasped for air. Waiting a beat to clear his head, he tucked his legs to the side and pushed himself onto his knees and then his feet. His vision blurred. A dizzy spell clouded him. Inhaling slowly, he wobbled in place until the world settled.

The fake Milena strutted in front of him. *Guide me home.*

He staggered forward.

Hagano shuffled through the streets. Milena paused from time to time, looking back as she waited for him to catch up. The lack of people cast an eerie aura over the city, as if ghosts were watching him from every window. He expected his efforts to drain what little energy remained within him, but the more he walked, the more he livened. What had felt like complete emptiness now felt only half-empty.

He kept his eyes on the bird. Milena's temperament had always been a nuisance. She pecked at everyone, especially him. It didn't take long for Hagano to give up on liking her. But now, after her death, she brought him comfort. Her duplicate gave him a piece of home. She kept him company. She walked in front of him, pulling him home—towards his family. She kept him alive.

A bad step swept Hagano's feet out from under him. He crashed onto his knees and then toppled to his side. Milena's copy vanished. He tried to sit back up, but his head spun. He rolled onto his back. The fall robbed him of his growing strength.

Hagano looked around for any sense of where he was. The temple's steeple, The Sky Spear, came into view. Regardless of location, it always served as a guiding post. He guessed that at his current pace, it would take several hours before he reached his front door. He willed another Milena into existence, but it vanished. He tried again. Same result. With each attempt, it felt as if his power emptied as quickly as his strength.

A rumbling shook the ground, rattling his body. The movement awakened the nerves in his arms. Waves of sharp pains rippled over him like jagged teeth. The colossal Sky Spear leaned like a felled tree, sinking into the skyline. Terrestrial thunder bellowed. The loss of the Sky Spear implied one thing—the guards were losing.

Loneliness pierced him. His family had no inkling of his peril. His allies were scattered or killed. Ecret could offer him no aid. Even

Milena, fake or not, had left. The weight of solitude pushed down on his spirit.

No. He cleared his throat. The dread of defeat closed in on him, but he focused on the nameless feeling that told him to fight. The sight of Milena's eyes blocked out his fears. *This isn't how it ends. I can still fight. Ecret told me I could save myself.* A stabbing pain cut into his arms, making them twitch. He winced. *I still have myself.* The thought stirred his heart. *What can I do? Cry? Die? Fail? No amount of chickens would make a difference. What else is there?* Click—an idea struck. His eyes widened.

Lying prone, he lifted the stub of his arm to his lips. It trembled as he pulled it to his mouth. Lifting his head, he put his lips on his arm. His tongue caught a taste of the lingering tar. It burned—both his arms and his lips. The thought of ingesting it made him spit. The stub of the arm wouldn't be usable. He strained his neck to reach for his bicep, but he couldn't shake free the sleeve of his shirt. He grunted and relaxed both his arm and his neck.

Trying to get his foot to his mouth sounded impossible. *What else is there?*

Nothing came to mind. He bit his lip to ponder. Click. A thought made him cringe, but he only needed a piece—a small piece. Hagano tested the feel of his bottom lip between his teeth. No. Too daunting. He tried feeling the tip of his tongue between his incisors. Too uncomfortable. He pulled in a piece of cheek between his molars. Not even slightly better. If anything, mashing his cheek between his molars felt like the worst option.

Instinct begged him to not harm himself, but he pulled a small piece of his lip between his front teeth. With some fiddling, the amount of flesh felt right. It needed to be large enough to bite off and swallow in order to activate his power. He wasn't sure if it was possible to have too small of a piece for the power to work, but experimenting with his own lip and own pain was not an appealing time to figure that out. It was better to take in a sizeable amount and hope for the best.

The anticipation of eating his own flesh made him gag, but

desperation squelched the reflex. If he gagged, he might vomit it out and would need to start over. He readied himself with a few deep breaths. *Bite quickly, swallow quickly.* He didn't know if he could regrow parts of the body without making the whole, but what other choice was there?

Hagano chomped down as hard as he could. His jaw slipped, leaving his lip pinched, but not cut. Mouth closed, Hagano groaned until the pain subsided. It hurt, but felt miniscule compared to his arms.

Controlling his breath and suppressing his thoughts, he pulled his lip between his canines and swiftly bit down a second time. A tooth caught a piece of lip, cutting into it, but failed to sever an entire chunk. Blood spilt into his mouth. A surge of pain took hold for a brief moment. But the cut gave him a starting point. He bit into the same spot with the same canines as before. The gash in his lip widened, but remained attached. Hagano placed his lip for a final bite and clamped down. A piece tore off.

He gagged. His body heaved. Hagano pictured Milena's eyes and swept the piece of his lip to the roof of his mouth and forced himself to swallow.

The fear of failing idled at the back of his mind. It didn't matter. No sense in not trying to regrow his arms.

He conjured the memory of a burnt taste on his tongue and feathers on his hands. It felt odd, not having hands, but recalling the feeling of soft feathers brushing them.

"Heal." He could see the circle of fish swirling around Inturon's paw in the pond—the moment both Hagano and Ecret learned how to use this power. He couldn't just say the words to see if they would happen. He had to command the flesh to make them happen. *Heal!*

The wounds in his mouth faded as new flesh patched his lip and bleeding gums. The broken tooth repaired itself. The acidic wounds on his face vanished, taking the prickling pain with them. Blood returned to his system. Hagano's head cleared, making the world around him settle. The healing felt like the prickling of nerves—like a foot that had fallen asleep.

But his arms did not return.

Heal! Panic rose in his chest as he watched the ends of his arms fail to regenerate. His bad shoulder stung the same as it had for months. "Heal!" The pain in his biceps lessened, but remained. *No. Please.*

His heart raced. *Heal. Heal. Heal!*

Nothing.

He closed his eyes. A ball sank into his stomach. Whatever limit his power had, he'd reached it. Hagano couldn't get Ecret's gift to work as he hoped.

Come back. Another Milena spun into existence. She clucked.

He pushed himself onto his feet. Standing went smoother now that moving no longer made him light-headed. He examined what remained of his arms. The dried tar on his elbows boiled anew, seemingly unsettled again. It fought against a wave of new skin that his power tried to create, but the two powers looked equally matched—neither of them gaining ground. If he hoped to regain his arms, he'd have to clear his body of the tar.

A river ran through the city, not far from where he stood. If anything could dissolve the tar and clear his body of it, it would be the river. He jogged through the streets, guessing which turns would create the shortest path until the water came into view. He wanted to jump straight in, but held back. If he failed to regrow his arms, he needed to make sure he'd be able to get back on dry land.

Walls and buildings surrounded the river, extending down to the water's surface about ten feet. If he jumped in, he'd have to have to swim downstream to get out. His eyes wandered as he mulled over his options until catching a glimpse of a staircase. Whether by luck or divine intervention, the stairs rose out of the water across the bank less than a block away.

He jumped.

The cool rush of the river enveloped him. The tar protested as it rekindled his pain. It bubbled and stretched, fighting to hold its shape and stay attached. The melted ends of his muscles flared. Bits of the tar dug into them, burning anew.

Hagano kicked himself to the surface.

"Heal." He took in a deep breath. *Heal!* The nerves in his muscles prickled, but his arms did not reform. Skin from his upper arm wrapped around the open wound, sealing off the broken bone and tattered muscles. A surge of panic hit him. The tar was still inside him and his arms did not reform. Did he miss something in Inturon's instructions? Did he somehow misunderstand how to use the power? "Heal!"

Nothing changed.

Hagano kicked and flailed over to the steps. He flopped onto the stones, his legs still submerged. The clumsy thrashing of his armless swim sapped him of what little strength he had. He panted.

With pieces of tar now sealed inside him, his only thought was to eat more of his own flesh. Perhaps that would allow his gift to over-power the tar. But how big of a piece would he need? An arm's worth? The power clearly had limits, but what those were remained a mystery. He rolled over and stood.

The clicks and whir of interlocking thoughts brought a new idea to mind. He looked around for any sign of people, but saw no one. Staring at the steps, he focused on one thing. *Make... another... me.*

A human body swirled into existence and promptly fell over the steps. "Ugh. Naked." Hagano cringed and looked around. "At least it has arms."

No imperfections marked the body. No scars, no dirt, no blemishes. But no life filled it either. Its eyes stared off into the distance, expressionless.

For a split second, Hagano felt a bit self-conscious looking at a perfect version of himself. It had both arms. The left one hadn't weakened from months of going unused. But it was the small things that felt strangest. It didn't breathe. It didn't blink. There were no acne scars. No calluses. No... history.

Hagano prodded the duplicate, checking to see if it would somehow awaken. No response. He hoped that creating a whole copy of himself would reveal whether or not his power could make enough human flesh to create arms. It could. But still, the tar kept him from regenerating. He hung his head. The lifelessness of the body seemed like another clue, but to what, he didn't know. Every chicken he'd made so far was alive in some sense or another. This other Hagano wasn't though.

"Stand."

It held still without so much as a flinch.

Creating an army of himself wasn't an option—not that he wanted to unleash a naked squad of Haganos on the world. He walked up a few steps, intending to return home, but paused. Abandoning what looked like a dead version of himself felt wrong. He didn't want anyone to find it—especially Alessi. But he hadn't yet figured out how to get rid of what he created. "Vanish."

Nothing.

The chickens had disappeared when struck. Killing them might be the only way to undo them. He put a foot on the duplicate's chest, thinking that he might push it into the river until it drowned. But it didn't breathe, so it wouldn't drown. He'd have to... crush its head. He shuttered. Violently attacking what was essentially him made him queasy. But whoever found the body would have an uncomfortable understanding of what Hagano looked like without clothes.

He lightly placed his foot over the body's forehead and shook his head. "This is the weirdest." With a few short breathes, he lifted his foot and stomped. The body vanished. He sighed. *Glad that's over.*

Climbing the stairs, one thought prevailed—he needed more weapons. Two ideas sprang to mind, one at home and one at the temple courtyard.

The thought of seeing his family's faces again warmed him. But the feeling chilled. He didn't want his parents to see him in this condition. The horrors of his injuries would only flood them with pain. He didn't need that right now. It wouldn't help him in the fight to come. But their presence, their love, their support would comfort him. That is what he needed—in what felt like a selfish way.

He looked in the direction he thought pointed home. The bear pelt spread over his bed called to him.

CHAPTER SIXTEEN

SIX CHIMES

Hagano jogged through the streets towards his home for as long as his tired legs would carry him. They wore out quickly, leaving him to walk intermittently between short bursts of energy. His heart beat wildly. Blood pulsed in his injured shoulder and the stubs of his arms. Had his power not sealed his wounds in the river, he'd have bled out by now.

Homes sat abandoned with doors left ajar and windows cracked open, proof that they would never be reclaimed. It looked as if half the city evacuated, but to where, Hagano couldn't guess.

Other houses were locked up entirely as if closed curtains would withhold the enemy. A handful of doors were painted black with a knife stabbed into them. It made no sense at first until one of the doors also carried a message: Servants of the king.

"Traitors." Hagano spat at the door, wishing he could withdraw the knife and wipe away the message. But he kept moving, sweeping through a dozen blocks before the sight of another person jolted him. His feet fumbled over each other. He moved his arm as if trying to hold a hand to his chest.

An old man sat in a chair on his porch, smoking a pipe. They locked eyes. The man nodded, but showed almost no interest in the world around him. His gaze didn't threaten Hagano, nor did it welcome him. Only a determined look found its way into the man's expressions as if he didn't know what to make of a near armless boy.

Is he crazy? Or fearless?

The man glanced at Hagano's arms. "You don't look so good." He let out a puff of smoke and grumbled. "I don't imagine I'd have much trouble keeping you from my belongings." His hand fell to his side and patted the knife strapped to his hip.

Hagano tilted his head. "I'm not interested in robbing you."

"Good." The man crossed his legs. "Getting tired of scaring off looters." He blew a ring of smoke. "I'm sure you guards have bigger worries right now."

Hagano smiled—he'd never been called a guard before. "Us guards?"

The old man pointed a crooked finger at the sheath on Hagano's side. "Your friend went off that way, if that's who you're looking for."

"I'm sorry?" Hagano blinked, stumped by what the man meant.

"Another guard. A woman." He wagged his finger toward a nearby road. "She was being chased by a couple of strange people. Figured she was a guard." He puffed another ring of smoke. "Figured you are too with the black clothes and all."

A couple of people? Hagano swallowed. *Jaga.* Hagano pointed down the road with the stub of his arm. "This way?"

"Yessir." The old man sucked on his pipe. "Headed toward the river."

Water. Hagano started up a sprint and called back as he ran, "Thank you."

Of course, Jaga would go to the river. It was the most surefire way to gain an advantage—especially since she was outnumbered.

A flock of chickens swirled into being at Hagano's feet. They ran with him, or at least tried. *Find Jaga.* The birds spread out, heading in every direction and down every street as they made their way to the water's edge. *If you see her, make as much noise as possible.* Beads of sweat rolled down his brow. Ecret willing, if she was still alive, the sight of chickens would tell Jaga Hagano was on his way. He hoped the idea of him would be comforting. Something told him it might be burdensome.

Hagano cut through streets, taking turns as fast as possible. The riverbank came into view. He whipped around, searching every corner for any sight of her, but finding no one. *Listen.* He closed his eyes. The sounds of his heavy breathing nearly drowned out the world.

Panicked squawks echoed.

His eyes shot open—the sound pulling his attention downstream, past a bend in the river where Hagano couldn't see. He ran. *Protect her.*

His legs moved as fast as they could, his body weak. The path along the river took a sharp turn, making Hagano stop and change directions. The sight of a bloodied Jaga, sitting against a house, greeted him. His heart sank.

A flailing sylph lay face down on the cobblestone. A metallic prison trapped his legs. He tried to push himself up, but couldn't free the lower half of his body from the metal that wrapped tightly around it. Flashes of people ambushed him. Their spectral hands knocked Hagano against a wall. His head smacked against a wooden pillar, dizzying him. He shook his head, but couldn't see what force struck him.

The chickens circled Jaga, hopping and flapping wildly. Her eyes fluttered open, looking as if the noise woke her from death. Blood covered half her face. Mud caked her clothes.

"Jaga!" Hagano yelled. He rushed to her side, avoiding who he now knew was the lemur-faced man. Did his presence mean Alessi had been defeated? He shook his head. He didn't have time to stop and worry. "Jaga, can you walk?"

"Hagano?" The words barely made it out of her mouth.

"Yes, it's me. I'm here. You're gonna need to get up. I can't lift you."

"Your arms." She coughed.

"I know. Just try and get up." Hagano looked back to the man, afraid that the ghosts would free him and come attacking.

The lemur-faced man jerked his neck, his black and white eyes locking on Hagano. A chill washed over him. Flashes of ghosts revealed that they were trying to peel back the metal casing around the man's legs, but failing.

"My leg's broken." Jaga grabbed her thigh, just above a bleeding wound.

Hagano's heart sank. If she couldn't walk and he couldn't carry her, there was no way to get her to safety. Putting her on his back wouldn't work. He didn't have arms to hold her in place and she couldn't hold herself with her legs. The only way he could think of was to sling her over his good shoulder. It wouldn't be comfortable, or easy, but it might work. "Stand up on your good leg. I'm gonna put you on my shoulder."

Jaga nodded. She took hold of Hagano's shoulder as he bent over and the two managed to stand her up. He knelt down so she could position herself. With some fiddling, Hagano slowly stood up—careful to not drop Jaga. He tried to use what was left of his arms to keep her balanced, but it wasn't enough to make a difference. Upside down, she grabbed onto his waist to steady herself.

The first step felt wobbly. The second less so. Little by little, Hagano gained the confidence to walk while balancing her.

The lemur-faced man said nothing as they departed. For unclear reasons, the ghosts let them leave.

Hagano wanted to look back, make sure the man was still trapped, but didn't. Every movement had a risk of losing Jaga and their march was precarious enough.

Home. That was the only place Hagano could think to take her. He needed to go there anyway. His jaw clenched, thinking of how his mother would respond—undoubtedly distraught by his injuries. A wounded stranger shouldn't be too much more of a problem.

Their pace was slow. The trek felt endless. Hagano's mind began to wander, forcing him to remind himself to focus.

"Stop." Jaga's weak voice found its way to Hagano's ears.

Hagano paused. "What's wrong?"

"Just listen for a moment."

The hush of a breeze passed by. The tapping of chicken nails on cobblestone surrounded them as his flock moved about.

He commanded them to freeze. "I don't hear anything."

"Shhh." Jaga's hands pushed against his back. "Put me down."

He crouched. She slid off and sat down.

The faint echo of a chime rang.

"Chimes?" Hagano turned, looking for the source.

"Just listen." Jaga held still and closed her eyes.

Another chime rang. Then another. They stopped.

"I don't understand." Hagano whispered, fearing that Jaga still wanted him to be quiet.

"Six." She nodded. "Six chimes." The tension in her brow dispersed. "It's Inturon, the endling." She looked up at him, smiling. "There's hope after all."

He stood back. His lip twitched, wanting to grin back at her. "Are you sure?"

Another chime rang. Then another until six more rang out in succession.

Jaga nodded. "Six notes of a chime announce the arrival of an envoy from Inturon." She took a deep breath and gripped her leg.

"I've never heard—"

"Go see if you can see the procession ringing the chimes." She looked around and pointed toward a staircase on the outside of a nearby building.

Something sat funny. Hagano's gut told him something was wrong, but he didn't know what the feeling meant. "You're okay here?"

She nodded.

Hagano jogged to the stairs and made his way to the roof. It wasn't the tallest building in the area, but it gave him enough of a view to see out over the main road. The Sky Spear lay fallen over the city, half-crumbled from its collapse. His eyes searched the distant temple plaza and made their way toward the city entrance.

A band of people, about six if Hagano could see clearly, walked along the main road. They were far, but he could see a cat-like man standing in the middle. *Inturon?* Five people held up chimes, striking them in unison. Their tinkling rang out, louder than he would have thought possible.

With unfettered steps, the procession headed for the temple.

Hagano shook his head. Something was off. The Sylph King went into the temple after the attack to look for Inturon, the bearcat god. But Inturon just now entered the city. Was The Sylph King mistaken?

A click in his mind connected two thoughts. Lowell's story about the chimpanzees—how one would walk into another's territory and be ambushed. He said that the ambushers would cannibalize the young... and Inturon was the youngest god.

Knots twisted Hagano's stomach. He tried to yell out to the young god, but his voice was hoarse. He swallowed what felt like a lump.

He's walking into a trap.

CHAPTER SEVENTEEN

HEIRLOOMS

Hagano leaned as he walked, balancing Jaga over his one good shoulder. Neither of them knew how to warn Inturon of The Sylph King's trap. Another battle was about to unfold inside the temple walls. For now, Hagano could only hope it wouldn't result in the death of another god.

Nearing home, Hagano tried to pick up his sluggish pace. The familiar sight of his neighborhood brought both comfort and dread. A guilt loomed. He was about to shatter his parents' world—again. He didn't want to imagine their reaction to his missing arms or the fact he didn't know Alessi's whereabouts or wellbeing. But it didn't matter how little he wanted to hurt them. What had happened, happened. Hagano couldn't change it. Neither could his parents. The only path forward was to accept reality.

Down the road, he could see his mother whittling away at a stick. The sight of her made his stomach plunge into his feet. Something about her constant care made him want to crawl into bed, sleep off his worries, and leave the rest to her.

His mother sat in a chair, bouncing her leg as she often did when her nerves couldn't calm. She looked almost manic as she swiped the blade across the wood, shaving off pieces as if she were peeling an onion.

"Mom!" he called, half hobbling, half jogging.

His mother shot to her feet. She threw the wood and knife to the ground and dashed towards Hagano, faster than he thought possible in her old age and diminishing health. "Hagano." Her face flushed red. A stream of tears ran down her cheeks.

"Take her." Hagano approached his mother and slumped Jaga off his shoulder. He too started to cry, not knowing exactly why.

His mother ducked under Jaga's arm and steadied her. "What happened to you?" She looked her son up and down. "You're arms. You're hurt. What happened? Are you in pain?" Her voice shook as emotion took over. "Your arms. I don't understand—they look healed."

Hagano shook his head. "I'm not in pain." He gestured to Jaga. "But she is. Her leg is broken and she's lost a lot of blood." His voice cracked. "Help me take her inside."

His mother nodded and started for the house. "Your arms," she repeated, still in disbelief. "You... what happened?"

"I ... I...." He strained for breath, not realizing how much he was crying. "I was attacked, but Ecret..." He wanted to say his god had come to his rescue, but that wasn't exactly true. The power saved him —Ecret's power—but only after the god told him face to face that only Hagano would be able to save his own life. The memories jumbled together, feeling like a nonsense he wouldn't be able to explain. He swallowed. "I saw you whittling." He managed a laugh between sobs. "You only do that when you're too anxious to do anything else."

"That's not true." She limped along the road, balancing Jaga.

Hagano made a weak attempt to smile. "Last time I saw you whittling was when your niece was in labor. I think you carved some sort of potato monster."

"It was a sheep." She adjusted Jaga's weight. "And it was going to be the baby's first toy."

"It was really ugly."

"Don't be mean to me and tell me what is happening." She frowned for split second before shooting Hagano a knowing look. "You're trying to distract me, aren't you?"

"Was it that obvious?"

"Do you have any idea how worried I've been? I couldn't sleep. You've been gone for over a day. The Sky Spear collapsed. I've been going absolutely mad." She sniffled and wiped her nose with the back of her hand. "Now look at you. You're here and your arms are..." Biting her lip, she scrunched her face as if she were about to burst into tears. "What happened?"

His mind jumped from the burning library, to fighting Lowell, to losing his arms. *It's only been a day?* His mother's words caught up to him. He hadn't been unconscious for long. "Let's get her settled and then I'll explain. But I'm okay. I promise. I know I don't look it, but I'm fine." He sniffed. "I also..." He cleared his throat and played with his jaw. "I won't be here long."

"What?" His mother's expression hardened. "No. You can't go."

Hagano shook his head. "Mom, Ecret has more work for me to do."

She blanched. Hagano's mother was a woman of faith, but he could see in her eyes that she didn't know how to accept the idea that Ecret would put her son in danger. The dissonance kept her silent, but the fear on her face felt louder than thunder.

Nearing the door, she yelled inside, "Pyotr! Come help." She led Jaga through the door where Hagano's father met them, looking pale and baggy-eyed.

"What is going on, Elise?" He stared at his son's missing arms. "Hagano?"

"Just help mom get Jaga to your bed."

His father handed his cane to Jaga, who took it with a quiet, "Thank you."

He escorted her to the bedroom before returning to fetch a cup of water and disappearing back into the bedroom.

His mother followed her husband. She placed a loving hand on her son's face, "Let's get you in bed. Then I'll fetch a doctor."

"I'm not in pain. And I need to leave."

His mother held tight to Hagano's shirt. "You can't. You don't know what you're saying."

"No, mom. I told you, Ecret has more work for me to do."

She shook her head. "You can't. You need to rest. Someone else can do it. We'll have Alessi take care of it."

His father came back to the kitchen. "Have you seen him?" He leaned his weight on the table as he sat down in a chair.

Hagano shook his head. "Have you?"

"He'll be back soon." His mother tried to pull Hagano to another chair at the table, but he wouldn't budge.

"I need the bear skin pelt in my room." Hagano stepped back, freeing him from his mother's grip.

"Yes. That will make you comfortable." She started for his room.

"No, mom. This is going to sound a bit mad, but I need to eat a piece of it."

His mother turned back to him. "What are you saying, Hagano?" She looked to her husband. "Are you just going to stand there?"

"Mom, look." Hagano lifted his chin to point at the end of the kitchen table. A chicken appeared out of nowhere.

Milena's appearance put a hush over the room.

"Ecret gave me a power." Hagano struggled to find the words. "It's... it's a power to create animals, any animal whose flesh I have eaten since the attack. I know it's hard to understand."

The copy of Milena strutted around the kitchen table, clucking.

His mother pointed at the chicken, her mouth gaping. "We ate that chicken."

"Let's eat it again." His father reached out to pet Milena.

"They're not actual chickens, dad."

"They?" His mother asked.

"Oh, yeah." Hagano reached to the table, creating a second hen, then a third, fourth, and fifth. "I can make lots of them. Because of Ecret."

"He gave you this power?" His mother walked to the table and looked over the chickens.

"Yes." Hagano relaxed.

His parents' eyes wandered as they each nodded to themselves—the first sign that they finally understood what he was trying to say.

Hagano took a deep breath. "But I need something more useful than chickens. I have a bear pelt in my room. Does anyone have anything else? Some piece of animal flesh that I can eat and use?"

His parents exchanged frowns.

A labored groan sounded from his parents' room. Hagano turned to face it. "Jaga, are you alright?"

"Yes, just... settling." Her voice was weak.

Hagano looked back to his mother, then to his father. He wasn't sure if they were thinking about what they might have to help or were staying quiet because they didn't want him to leave. "I know this is scary, but *think*. What do we have? You can't get distracted. I need you." Another wave of tears rolled down his face. "I need you to help me. Ecret's life depends on it."

More silence.

"Please." He took in a quick breath. "Please, help—"

"Your father has some rabbit fur in the bedroom." His mother hustled off as fast as she could. "I'll fetch it and check on Jaga."

"I can't think of anything." His father lifted himself to his feet.

"That's okay." Hagano licked his lips, tasting the salt of his tears. "I need you to cut off a piece of that pelt." He headed for his room, but stopped in front of the door as soon as he realized he didn't have hands to open it.

His father retrieved a knife and opened the door for his son. He braced himself against the wall before sitting on the bed. He took the knife to the corner of the bear pelt and haphazardly cut off a piece.

Hagano sat down next to him.

His father offered him the small, furry piece of bear skin.

One look at the pelt made Hagano cringe. He could already feel the bristly fur tickling his throat. "Would you mind folding it up a little so it's not so big?"

Nodding, his father folded it over itself, trying to cover the fur and make it smaller before placing it in Hagano's mouth.

Rough textures met his tongue before transforming into the taste of burnt meat. It made no sense—the pelt hadn't been burnt. The taste conjured the memory of the chicken stew, which also tasted charred at first. He hummed to himself, thinking the taste might be connected to his power.

Staring at his feet, he tried to not think about swallowing the pelt. He wanted to plug his nose before gulping it down, but his lack of hands was starting to register. With a deep breath, he forced it down. His gut wrenched, wanting to gag. He flexed his toes in hopes of distracting himself. The urge to vomit faded.

Looking at an empty corner of the room, Hagano willed a bear into existence. It snapped into being.

His father gasped. "Oh... that's... nice."

"Thanks?" Relief washed over Hagano. His power was working.

The bear blankly scanned the room.

Hagano approached it with caution even though he knew it wouldn't harm him. Even on all fours, the height of the animal came to Hagano's chest. He reached towards the bear with the end of his arm and brushed its head. Hagano pressed his face into the fur. "This is so much better than a chicken."

"Oh, majesty!" His mother clutched her chest as she walked into the room. "That thing's going to break something." She was met with a bug-eyed glare from Hagano. "Well, it's no bear, but here is a rabbit pelt." She held it out in front of Hagano. "And this." She opened her fist, revealing a pearl necklace in her palm.

"Thank you." His parents coming together to help him gave him more joy than he anticipated. They also seemed to be handling the situation with surprising calm—a sign of their strong faith. Something about their trust in Ecret made Hagano feel more secure. He wasn't crazy for believing in his god. That or they were all insane.

His father took the rabbit pelt and cut away a piece of it. Once again, he rolled up the pelt and put it in Hagano's mouth.

Hagano took it somewhat begrudgingly. He couldn't imagine the need of rabbits after arming himself with bears, but there was no sense in not taking it. He swallowed without gagging, which surprised him.

His mother held the pearls in front of him.

Hagano shot her a sympathetic look. "Pearls aren't actually a part of a clam, but thank you." He fought back a groan. If rabbits were pointless, clams would be doubly so anyway.

She frowned. "Oh... wait!" She abruptly left for the kitchen and returned with an old pipe.

"What are you doing with that?" His father gave a disquieted gasp.

Pointing to the mouthpiece, his mother's eyes lit up. "It's made from ivory."

"That's perfect." Hagano smirked. His hope of storming the temple with an army of beasts might be coming true after all. Returning to the temple started to feel less and less like a suicide mission.

She broke off a chunk of the pipe's ivory mouthpiece. A guttural yelp escaped his father's mouth, undoubtedly caused by seeing his favorite pipe ruined.

The ivory felt like a rock sliding down Hagano's throat. For a brief moment, he worried how he would pass it, but that would be a problem for later. Ready to test his newfound animals, Hagano made a rabbit and had it hop around the bed.

"Don't put an elephant in here." His mother dropped the rest of the pipe on the bed.

"I wasn't going to." Hagano grinned at her, happy to see her worry about the house and not his missing arms. "Okay. Does anyone have anything else?"

Everyone looked at each other. His father shrugged. His mother shook her head.

Plops, their old mutt, strutted into the room and sat down in a puddle of its own flabby skin.

His mother looked at the dog, then to Hagano.

"Uh." Hagano bit his lower lip. "No."

"Then that's it." She clasped her hands together.

The idea to stay with his family tempted him. After nearly being killed several times and losing his arms, the only thing he yearned for was the peace of home. But he didn't know the fate of his god or his brother and couldn't stand the thought of leaving them in their time of need. His master and his family both armed him with everything they could. They sacrificed for him and if Hagano didn't rise to the occasion, it would all be in vain.

Hagano sent the bear out of his room and the house.

"Wait just a moment." His mother fetched Hagano a tall mug of water and a rice patty. "Sorry I don't have more to eat."

"I couldn't ask for more."

She fed him the rice patty and helped him drink.

After finishing the last bite, Hagano looked down the hall to his parents' bedroom. "I need to say goodbye to Jaga."

His mother nodded and led him to her room. She opened the door and left it ajar so he could let himself out.

"I heard everything." Jaga rolled her head to where she could see him.

"I have a lot more than chickens now." Hagano tried to laugh. It sounded forced.

Jaga's breathing shortened. "I need you to bring Ecret back, Hagano. I can't fight anymore."

"You've done enough."

"If you... if Ecret is lost..." Jaga paused. Her cheeks reddened. "I will never see my husband again. Or my daughter." Jaga took a few shallow breaths. "Her name is Valpuri. She died two weeks after I gave birth." Her bottom lip trembled. She wiped her eyes with a sleeve. "My husband... the sadness took him." She paused again. "If Ecret is lost and I can't meet them in paradise, then I should have let it take me too." Closing her eyes, she turned away.

Words escaped Hagano. Everything that sprang to mind fell short of what hope he could offer. He bowed his head. "I will bring Ecret back." Something about his quivering tone made him think she wouldn't believe him. He wasn't sure he believed himself. "And one day, he will take you to your family. I promise."

Neither of them moved as they shared a quiet moment.

"I should go." He inched toward the door, keeping an eye on her in case she had anything more to say. He wanted to thank her for saving him at the library, but thought that might sound too much like a goodbye. "I'll be back."

Leaving the room, he rejoined his parents and the bear outside.

His mother wrapped her arms around her son. "Are you sure?"

"Yes." Hagano bit his lip.

Ecretians. A voice echoed in his head—not his, not Ecret's, and not the one that kept telling him to eat.

His mother pulled back and looked at her husband.

He shrugged. "Did you hear that?"

Hagano and his mother nodded in unison.

I am Inturon, the endling, and Lord Ecret's brother.

The stubs of Hagano's arms stung like lightning, making his muscles cramp. "Ah." He pulled them close to his body hoping to relieve the pain.

News of my brother's demise brought me here. I am sorry for your loss. I share it with you. But do not be afraid. I will avenge my brother and bring you under my protection.

"I should go." Hagano hadn't told his parents of The Sylph King's trap.

"Still?" His mother put a hand on his arm. "Inturon is here. He will take care of everything."

Shaking his head, he pulled away. "I'm sorry. I must do as Ecret instructed and go back to the temple."

She wrapped herself in a hug. Hagano's father joined her and sent him off with a curt nod.

Hagano walked away, the bear in tow. One thought occupied him —Inturon would save the people, but Hagano would save Inturon.

CHAPTER EIGHTEEN
A PARADOX APOLOGY

The sun hung low in the sky, casting long shadows over the city. The heat of the day faded, welcoming a cool evening breeze. Hagano followed the main road, beelining to the temple plaza. Soft thumping followed as the bear behind him stepped with the weight of a boulder.

Chickens, bears, rabbits, and elephants now waited his command to snap into being and fight for his cause. He hummed to himself. The limits of his powers were still a mystery. Something told him they weren't boundless. He'd need to test them and he'd better do it before a moment of need. But one more weapon waited on the temple steps —if his hunch was right.

The festival musicians included a group of drummers. If he weren't mistaken, those drums were made from a wooden base and stretched crocodile skin. With any luck, he was right and the drums were still there. He shook his head—who would have moved them anyway?

Alessi. His brother's name kept popping up in his thoughts. Last Hagano had seen him, he still had arms and Alessi was fighting the lemur-faced man inside the temple walls. There'd been no word from him since and the lemur-faced man was trapped by Jaga—a sign that

Alessi may have lost that fight. Alessi had run to their parents' house after the attack to check on Hagano, but he hadn't shown up again. At least, not yet. A chilling guilt sunk into him. What if he were in the streets, dying, like Jaga?

He sniffed. *Don't think like that.* As far as he knew, Inturon had reached the temple and was already at work saving everyone— including Alessi. And Inturon was immortal. *But so was Ecret.* Hagano picked up his pace.

His highest priority was warning Inturon about The Sylph King's trap. Although, he didn't know what the trap was. His brain felt fuzzy. Something didn't add up. It was a feeling Hagano faced every time he got stuck on a puzzle. A link was missing. His gut knew it, but his mind hadn't been able to find it.

No matter. He'd inform Inturon about everything, then work to bring Ecret's body back inside the temple. That was the goal, right? At least according to Alessi. One of the guards had reached his book before the library burnt down and knew that's what Ecret wanted. *Hmm.* Fuzzy again.

Once Ecret's spirit returned to the body, then all he'd need to revive was the blood under the control of the cheetah-faced woman. The image of her face flashed in his mind. She'd killed the hiero-phants without breaking a sweat. Hagano's stomach tightened. How would he kill her? *Kill.* The word balled up in his throat. He'd have to kill someone. He sighed, trying not to think of her as a person. *Maybe an elephant could squash the blood out of her.*

Giant stone bricks lay scattered over the road. The fallen Sky Spear stretched out in front of him, blocking his path. The buildings under the steeple lay demolished. The steeple, though broken, kept its shape. Even on its side, it stood taller than most buildings.

Hagano peeked inside through a hole in the wall. The interior looked like nothing more than a broken staircase and a collection of relics thrown against a wall. A window offered a passageway through the tower.

A stone brick fell, sending up a puff of dust. The structure looked like it could crumble any moment, but there was no time to look for an alternate route.

Hagano tip-toed through the hole in the wall, across the room, and out the window. Turning back, he willed the bear to follow. Its monstrous size made it difficult to creep. It bumped up against a wall, knocking more loose bricks onto its head. Hagano winced, thinking the bear would dissipate. It didn't.

"Huh." He tilted his head. "Tougher than chickens."

As the two neared the plaza, Hagano took to the shadows. The last light of day began hiding behind the mountains.

At the plaza entrance, Hagano peeked around a corner to search for any signs of life. Nothing. At the base of the courtyard laid dozens of bodies, fanned out in a circle. Each of them had a slit throat. The sight made Hagano flinch. None of them showed burn marks, cuts, or any wounds from the battle. All of them wore the mark of the clergy. Their deaths were not the work of the enemy. They took their own lives.

The sight of them brought Jaga's words to the forefront of his mind. These people had watched their god die. They must have thought their spirits could catch up to Ecret in the afterlife if they acted fast enough. In their minds, it was their last chance for paradise.

The stench of the bodies reached Hagano. Not only were there those who killed themselves, there were also dozens, if not hundreds, of dead guards. Chunks of flesh, half eaten by tar, lay scattered across the grounds—rotting for nearly two days. Seeing the dead Ecretians made Hagano hold his breath, not only because they were killed, but because they were wearing festival clothes. He pictured them dressing up to celebrate their god, only to be murdered on what should have been one of the happiest days of the year.

He squinted, scanning the area where he thought the musicians played. A dozen drums sat undisturbed. He turned to the bear and put the stub of his arm on its head. *Stay.* Its movements were too clumsy and its body too large to move about with any amount of stealth.

You can do this. Just take the first step. He let out a long breath and stepped out of the darkened alleyway.

He crept over to the nearest drum, looking in every direction as if he knew someone would ambush him at any moment. The instrument was too cumbersome to try and move, with or without help. Other instruments littered the ground. He crouched next to the drum. The scaly texture of the lid put a grin on his face.

He pursed his lips. *How am I going to get a piece of the skin?* Leaning close, he bit onto the ledge. The bitter taste of dirt made his mouth feel like it was full of chalk. Ignoring the feeling, he chomped. The leathery skin resisted. Fiddling with his jaw, he bit down over and over without making a single puncture. He grunted.

Standing, he put his foot on the drum and hoped his weight would tear through it. The drum repelled him. "Ugh." He stomped his ankle onto the skin, thinking it would punch through. His foot bounced off. A low '*bm*' sounded and echoed around him.

Dumb. Dumb. Dumb. Dumb. Dumb. Dumb.

He crouched behind the drum. The thumping of his heart filled his ears. *That was so dumb!*

Lifting his chin, he scanned the area. No movement caught his eye. *Stupid, but lucky.* He'd have to use a bear. One way or another, it would tear off a piece of the drum.

A pebble knocked into his shoulder.

He froze—unable move. He wasn't breathing, but also didn't need to. He tried to look around, but his eyes were locked in place. It felt similar to when Ecret grabbed his face and time slowed. Only this time, he was still in his body. His movements didn't feel entirely halted, but he moved so slightly that it felt like they had.

A pair of feet appeared in Hagano's line of vision. He was looking down at the drum and now at a man crouching down to meet face to face. A white line was painted from the end of his nose up into his equally white hair. "Hello," he said with only a hint of a soft accent—the vowels pure. He waved pleasantly at Hagano like an old friend from across the room. "What a curious sight you are."

The man strutted around Hagano. "No arms? An old injury, I see.

But rather odd for someone wearing a sheath." He pulled the sheath from Hagano's side, unlocking it from the time distortion. "You're clearly focused on this drum for some reason." He kicked the drum, which gave off a low hum. "A handsome young man, though probably not much younger than I am." He patted Hagano's head. "Hm. Sweaty. And you're wearing the same clothes those annoying capitol guards had on. Someone's here for revenge. Am I right?" He prodded Hagano's forehead with a finger.

Hagano's control over himself returned. He stretched his back, testing his movements. "Um... hello." He wanted to call the bear to him, but strangely felt unthreatened. The man didn't act aggressive or even carry himself like the other animal-painted enemies.

"Am I right?" The man raised an eyebrow.

Hagano didn't want to admit that the man had figured him out. He had seen the puzzle pieces of the scene and put them in their proper places—drawing the correct conclusion. He couldn't admit that they were enemies. He didn't want to start a fight. But he couldn't think of a lie that would explain his behavior. As Hagano scrambled to think, he sat in silence and offered a blank stare.

The man looked around as if he found someone's lost child. "Do you speak Ecretian? I know mine is a bit rusty, but I didn't think it was *that* bad."

Say you're lost. No. *Tell him you're here for help.* No. Stupid. *Say something about Inturon.* But what?

Fuzzy. His brain felt fuzzy. He called the bear to him, commanding it to sneak up behind the man. He didn't know if bears stalked their prey, but it crawled closer and closer like a tiger nearing a kill.

The man sat cross legged on the ground in front of Hagano. He gestured for Hagano to sit too. "Please. Let's talk."

Hagano forced himself to keep his attention on the man as the bear crept closer. By what felt like a miracle, the man failed to notice anything. *Distract him.* "My name is Hagano."

"Oh." The man sounded startled, but pleased. "Good. It's nice to meet you. Well." He reached his hand out. "My name is Eachan."

With a short gasp, he snapped back his hand "So sorry, that was insensitive. Do forgive." He bowed his head. "Tell me, I'm curious, why were you trying to destroy a perfectly good drum? An animal had to die to make that, you know."

"Well..." Hagano thought, not knowing what he was about to say, but talking nonetheless. "Yes. You see..." He watched the bear get closer. It moved so slowly, it felt like it would never get to them, but he dared not make it move faster. "My grandfather..."

"Mother's dad or father's dad?" Eachan folded his arms.

Hagano fumbled over his words, "Fl-ff-uh-father's father. It's, um... yes. Sorry. Anyway. He's a drummer. Or *was* a drummer, one of..." Hagano waved his short arm at the line of drums. "Well, he was. Now he's dead." Hagano wanted to slap himself. He was going to die telling a remarkably fake story like a complete idiot.

Eachan's expression softened. "Did he die during your festival?"

"Yes." Hagano responded instantly, far too excited about how that made sense with what he was saying. "He did. He got... trampled. And he always wanted to be buried with a piece of his drum. So here I am."

"I'm very sorry." The tone of Eachan's voice sounded strangely sincere.

"You're sorry?" Hagano leaned forward, taken off guard by Eachan's apology.

"Yes. It may have been my fault. We knew there would be casualties, but we didn't actually want to hurt anyone. Other than Ecret, I mean. Obviously, that was intentional." Eachan put his hands on his knees and rocked forward.

Didn't want to hurt anyone? Hagano clenched his teeth. He could feel the muscles in his face tighten, but he tried not to look angered. Killing Ecret was the most damaging thing anyone could have possibly done. How could Eachan, an enemy, try to sympathize with Hagano now? It was insulting. Paradoxical. It made no sense. He felt fuzzy.

He exhaled softly, releasing a bit of frustration. For a split second, he considered the idea that Eachan was being genuine. Had the person sitting before Hagano also been swept up in forces far greater than him? He almost felt guilty that the bear finally reached the two and was swiping its massive claw into the back of Eachan's head.

The bear paw struck.

Eachan didn't move.

Frozen on impact, the paw and the bear held still.

Eachan turned his head towards the bear. "Hm. Soft." He grabbed the bear's arm and used it to bolster himself onto his feet. "Oh. This again." Eachan reached back behind him and withdrew two gloves with sharpened daggers for fingers. He slipped them on and turned to Hagano. "I'm honestly very sorry, but I'm going to have to kill you too." Eachan spun around, swiping the bear with his knifed-glove and sending it out of this world.

CHAPTER NINETEEN
EACHAN

Hagano rolled backwards away from Eachan. He flexed his toes, waiting for either of them to make the first move. He hadn't yet experimented with his power. Now he wished he had. Then he would know how many bears and how many elephants were at his disposal.

The word 'kill' echoed in his mind. He could command the bears to kill Eachan, but his stomach protested the thought. *Attack.* A trio of bears snapped into being at his sides.

They charged.

Eachan spun around, light on his feet, as if dancing. With a single swipe of the hand, he could stop a bear in time and slice it into oblivion. He reached left, killing a bear, then right, killing another, then behind him, killing the third. Over and over he slashed through them without suffering even the smallest scratch.

Hagano called three more, but held them back. Then another. Then a fifth. His mind reached out for more, but none came. Six? His dreams of an endless army stopped at the number six? He huffed. His horde of chickens at his disposal far exceeded six, but this was somehow different. His mind cleared—the puzzle of the battle had already started unfolding.

Eachan could slow things near the point of immobility. Hagano was also first frozen when a pebble hit him in the back. Did that mean Eachan could use his power vicariously?

Hoping for a moment to think, Hagano sent the bears to Eachan.

Eachan spun, kicking bears and slicing them until the last one vanished.

A fatigue struck Hagano. He panted, feeling as if someone had smacked the air out of him. Had Eachan stolen his breath? No. That would be a second power and Ecret dispelled the idea that a human could possess two. He swallowed. It must be the bears draining him.

Standing up straight, Eachan poised himself to strike. "We don't have to do this, you know. Just go home and forget about Ecret."

The offer seemed more appealing now that Hagano failed to land a single blow. "Or *you* could go home and forget about Ecret."

Eachan smiled. "Fair enough. So, just bears, huh?"

Hagano nodded. Leading Eachan to believe he could only make bears might provide an opportunity to catch him by surprise.

"And only six?" Eachan huffed, unimpressed.

Hagano's heart sank. Even while fighting off six hundred-pound beasts, Eachan managed an accurate summation of Hagano's power. He was much smarter than Lowell. Outwitting him would be much more difficult.

"The other guy could make about thirty, I think," Eachan added. "It was quite the nuisance."

"Other guy?" Hagano stepped back, ready to make more bears.

"The one who had this power before you." Eachan looked a bit dumbstruck at Hagano's question. "The head of your law enforcement. One of your hierophants. The... Hallux, I want to say." Eachan's eyes darted back and forth, looking as if he was trying to determine if he remembered correctly. He shrugged. "He was a good fighter. Obviously lost though."

"What do you mean by 'obviously'?" A tenseness gripped Hagano's bad shoulder, wakening the all-too-familiar pain.

"Because *you* have that power." Eachan's eyebrows twitched, making him look confused for a split second. "Did you not know that?" He waited for a response, but got none. "Ecret doesn't tell you much, does he?" Eachan smirked. "Excuse me, *did* he?"

Hagano's breaths shortened as he tried to fight off a panic. "Why don't *you* tell me?"

It seemed Eachan was telling the truth. Jaga had already told Hagano a power can only be given to one person at a time. Since Hagano had this one, the Hallux must have been dead. But why would Eachan volunteer this information? His mind felt fuzzy.

"Shall we?" Eachan fiddled with his gloves.

Hagano resummoned the bears. All six locked their gaze on Eachan. They slowly encircled their enemy, then stood on their hind feet. Hagano, even as the one controlling the animals, felt daunted by their might.

Eachan tried to keep an eye on each bear as they circled him.

A plan—Hagano needed a plan. The bears alone weren't doing anything and they were the only thing Eachan knew about. They would have to be his first line of defense. Anything else would only give away more information and weaken Hagano's position.

He could make plenty of chickens and probably rabbits, if his power balanced the amount of flesh he ate against the size of the beasts. *Hmm.* That was a thought. Perhaps the number of animals he could make was determined by their mass. It was the only explanation that made sense—at least in the moment.

His last trick would be an elephant—maybe two if he was lucky. They would be the hardest to kill, which hopefully meant Eachan wouldn't be able to handle them. He'd never made one before. Perhaps the piece of ivory he ate wouldn't even activate his power.

"Why did you kill Ecret?" Hagano decided once again to try and use Eachan's curiosity as a distraction. Deep down, he also just wanted some way to make sense of the whole catastrophe.

"The same reason you are here tonight, fighting, all for the glory of your god." Eachan rocked on his heels, looking almost bored.

"So The Sylph King is your god now?"

Eachan shrugged, seemingly unfazed by the idea of worshipping a tyrant. "We all worship something."

Some...thing? The odd choice of words felt funny, but maybe it was just a matter of Eachan's rusty Ecretian.

Eachan dashed out of the ring of bears. His arms grazed the sides of the two he passed, locking them in time. He leapt at Hagano, pulling back his arm and swinging it at Hagano's face.

Hagano blocked it with the paw of a new bear. It froze, then vanished.

With his other hand, Eachan swung at Hagano's neck. The tip of one of the gauntlet's blades paralyzed him and sliced open his throat with a single swipe.

Hagano could do nothing but feel the cold night air creep into his open throat. The wound didn't hurt—not yet. He didn't know how long he would be frozen, but as soon as he was released, he would need to heal the wound. He counted the seconds.

Three... Four... Five....

Eachan bowed to Hagano. "My apologies." He cut away each bear that raced towards him, leaving just one locked in place. Removing his gloves, he placed them back in a pouch hidden in his robes.

Twelve seconds passed and the bear whose arm blocked Eachan's strike unfroze and fell to the ground with a thud. Fifteen seconds. That's how long the temporal distortion lasted. Since the bear just unfroze, Hagano was about to unfreeze as well. He now had an advantage. Eachan put away his weapons and let his guard down. Hagano would have to act dead for a moment, which might mean waiting to heal his throat and endure the subsequent pain. The chance to surprise Eachan would be worth it though.

The power released Hagano. He collapsed to the ground. The sting of a sliced throat shocked him. Blood covered the wound and dripped down his shirt. Hagano regrew the flesh. The instant healing soothed him like a numbing balm. He wanted to cheer. The tar in his body hadn't prevented him from healing. It must be locked in his arms.

Footsteps thudded as Eachan walked away.

Hagano looked out to Eachan and commanded his power to drop a bear onto his head.

Nothing happened. His power wasn't listening.

Hagano tried again, focusing more, and thinking of only of this one desire.

Nothing. Was he too far? Was his power also limited by proximity? He thought back at the chickens and bears that had all appeared at his side. He would have to get close.

Hagano rolled onto his feet and crept toward Eachan. His heart raced with each step, certain that Eachan would look back at any second.

He didn't. He was only a few feet away.

Now.

A titanic bear fell from the sky. It hit Eachan's head, knocking him down, but stalling in the air mid-fall.

Eachan dropped to the dirt, but the bear did not crush him. It floated in the air, motionless.

Hagano created a second bear above the first. It fell onto the suspended one, pushing it down like a hammer on a nail. A third bear fell onto the frozen one, doubling the weight on it and pushing it towards a prone Eachan. Their weight made the frozen bear slowly inch towards him.

Eachan rolled out from under the suspended bear just to find another one soaring towards his face. It locked in place with the slightest touch. The unfrozen bears pounded their paws onto the second frozen one. Throwing their weight into their brother, they sent it inching towards Eachan, leaving him little room between the ground and the beast.

He rolled across the ground, slipping out from under the bears with just enough room to escape. "Such a nuisance." Eachan reached behind his back and withdrew his gauntlets.

Dozens of chickens swarmed him. He kicked at them, but just as soon as one vanished, another took its place.

The two free bears leapt at him.

He met one of their swipes with a swat of the hand and the other with a soft punch, seizing them both with his power.

Hagano ran at Eachan amidst a second flock of chickens. The first group cut off his enemy from escaping in one direction. So many birds flooded the streets, some immobilized, some not, that Eachan had to fight for a place to step. Hagano approached from the other direction, his birds covering the ground and two more bears running to Eachan's sides to flank him. Two frozen bears returned to normal and joined the fray.

Eachan climbed atop a still bear. The chickens hopped and flapped at its hind legs in a fruitless effort to get at Eachan. He slipped on his gloves. The moment more of the bears reached him, Eachan jumped off his perch, over one of the charging bears, and somersaulted onto his feet into a full charge towards Hagano. He brandished the knives on his hands and swung.

Hagano held out the stubs of his arms. One of Eachan's knives scratched Hagano, freezing him. Eachan took hold of Hagano's shoulder.

One by one, each of the six bears clawed at Eachan and froze just the same. With every threat trapped by his power, Eachan released Hagano from his grip. He removed a glove and stored it. He prodded Hagano every few seconds—renewing the hold over him. Eacahn removed a thin, but long rope from another pouch that hung inside his robes. He sighed. "Not sure how you survived a sliced throat, but no matter. *Something* will kill you."

The purpose of the rope wasn't yet clear. Before he could guess, his thoughts pulled him in a different direction. Eachan wasn't sure how Hagano survived the sliced throat. Did that mean the man who possessed the power before him wasn't able to heal himself?

He held back the chickens. Their pestering seemed to have lost its effect, but their presence could now be a distraction. *Go to the drums and fetch me a piece of crocodile skin.* He couldn't see the two chickens he'd commanded, but he had complete faith in their obedience.

"I don't care much for violence, Hagano." Eachan untied a knot in the rope and wrapped it around the necks of each bear. "I offered you the chance to leave." He tilted his head and met Hagano's eyes. "I offered the same chance to The Hallux."

He finished roping each bear and began tying a knot. Eachan

gripped the rope and closed his eyes. He inhaled loudly through his nose, held his breath, clenched his fist, and let go. A small surge of energy ran the course of the rope, vibrating it with a sharp buzz. Eachan reached into a pocket and pulled out a small stone. Another quick, but muffled buzz sounded from his fist. Then Eachan threw the stone at Hagano, hitting him squarely on the chest.

Hagano's heart would have raced if it were beating. Panic set in. His frozen bears could not come to his rescue. Chickens and rabbits seemed useless. He wasn't even sure he could make anything in his paralyzed state. He thought about trying an elephant, but even if he could, it could be rendered useless with the slightest touch.

"And yes, I killed him." Eachan shrugged. "But he tried to kill me first." He walked up to Hagano and shook his head with what looked like disappointment.

Hagano willed another chicken into existence between him and Eachan. It brushed against Eachan the moment it came to be. The chicken formed itself at an extremely slow pace. All of Hagano's creations had simply appeared, but this bird was fighting through Eachan's power. Hagano could see a bare embryo spin in the air. It morphed into a chick and then into a full-grown bird. It was like watching its whole life take place as it swirled in the air before him. Once grown, it stopped spinning and hung motionless.

Eachan swatted it away and stabbed his daggered glove into Hagano's chest. The knives cut around Hagano's heart. Eachan pulled his hand back and then plunged the knives into Hagano's chest once more. With a displeased look and clenched teeth, he twisted the blades around the heart.

The fear of failing to regenerate screamed at Hagano. His power managed smaller wounds, but could not remake his arms. Patching a giant hole in his chest felt beyond him.

Eachan tore out Hagano's heart and threw it on the ground. "Again, my apologies." Eachan spoke softly. "I'm not sure what it takes to kill you, but I suspect this will do."

Fifteen seconds was all that stood between Hagano and incomprehensible pain. He'd have to regenerate instantly, but what then?

Nothing he had tried had any effect. Eachan could take hold of him again and dissect him to bits until nothing remained.

Ten seconds remained.

The race towards death erased his thoughts. He didn't know how to fight anymore. He could try and run, but that might start a chase. And if Eachan could slow Hagano by throwing a stone, he'd never escape.

Five seconds.

His mind blanked. He needed his bears. All six were stationary. Whatever Eachan did to the rope kept them from unfreezing. His only hope was to heal himself and free his bears somehow.

One second.

Hagano unfroze. The hole in his chest sent an explosion of pain throughout his entire body. Collapsing to the ground, he nearly blacked out. A rush of relief flooded his core as his body regrew his heart and chest. A dying scream flew from his lips.

Eachan shook his head. "Impressive. You're apparently more resilient than Madigan." He raised a foot to slam it on Hagano's leg.

Hagano placed a chicken under Eachan's foot, causing him to not only miss Hagano, but lose his balance. While his enemy found his footing, Hagano slid away and sprinted towards the bears. He reached the semi-circle of beasts with no plan in mind on how to reclaim them.

Another rock struck his back. He couldn't move. He didn't have time to think about the inevitable torture that was coming his way. He focused his gaze on the bears in the faint hope that they would somehow know what to do. They were so close, but felt just as far as ever.

Eachan walked up to Hagano's side. "If not the heart, then maybe the brain? Or should I just cut you into a hundred pieces and see if you can pull yourself back together?"

Hagano called on his last hope, praying it would manifest. A thirteen-thousand-pound elephant dropped out of the sky. It crashed into the bears' heads, breaking their necks, and sending them away into the void from where Hagano could remake them. The rope still held its shape, freezing everything it touched—which was now just the mammoth.

Eachan recoiled.

Hagano placed his bears between him and his enemy. He held them back. He just needed to buy the time to regain control over his body.

By what felt like Ecret's grace, Eachan stood back.

Hagano unfroze. He walked out from behind the bears and the two men stared at each other as the breeze blew. A perplexed look crossed Eachan's face. Neither knew how to defeat the other.

The bears charged.

Eachan sat on the ground and closed his eyes.

The first bear to reach him tried to clobber him with two paws, but froze. The second came from the side, but failed to land a blow. The third, fourth, and fifth bears followed suit, surrounding Eachan, but falling prey to his power just the same. Without any room to strike, the final bear stalked around the huddle, waiting for the chance to attack. Even though the bears failed to strike, they successfully trapped Eachan between them.

Eachan's surrender made Hagano wary. He didn't see how his enemy could attack through the cage of bears. There was no way out and nothing to do but wait. It didn't seem likely that Eachan could turn the situation to his advantage, but something was amiss. His only guess was that Eachan wanted time to think.

The patter of chicken feet drew closer as one of Hagano's hens strutted up to him. It bent down and dropped a small piece of a drum at his feet.

"Finally," he whispered. It felt like ages ago that he sent a pair of chickens to the drum to peck away at the leather and bring back a piece. Now he had a new tool—crocodile. Hagano knelt down. The chicken picked up the piece of skin and placed it in his mouth. The exchange felt awkward, both having to position himself low enough to get the skin without any hands and also making the bird stick its beak into his mouth. After a bit of contorting, Hagano gulped down the gator skin and stood back up. He told his power to make a crocodile and watched intently as nothing happened. Confused, he tried again. Nothing. Something was wrong.

Hagano frowned. Using a crocodile in battle was, for some reason, not an option. Another idea sprang to mind. He summoned the one unfrozen bear to his side and directed it to search the dead guards for one of their swords and bring it back.

The bear sped away.

Hagano, again, tried to make a crocodile. Nothing happened.

"Are you not curious?" Eachan said from behind a wall of fur.

Hagano rolled his eyes, annoyed by Eachan's incessant chatting.

"I told you that a god regains his power when its mortal host dies. I also told you that I killed The Hallux."

"So?" Hagano groaned.

"Don't you get it? Ecret knew The Hallux had died." Eachan waited for a response. "Do I have to explain everything?"

The bear returned clumsily holding the hilt of a sword in its mouth. It was a moment Hagano wished he had the rest of his arms and could wield the sword himself. Instead, he would have to make due.

"Someone with The Hallux's powers doesn't just die—they're killed." Eachan's voice sounded muffled. "Only someone with a god-given power could take down The Hallux. Which means, when the power returned to Ecret, he knew his servant had been killed. The killing of one of Ecret's top servants means only one thing—war. Ecret knew an attack was coming."

"I don't believe you." Hagano tsked. Nothing Eachan said should hold any weight, but Hagano already knew Eachan had told him some truths. He had already confirmed what Jaga told him—that if Hagano had his power, it meant the previous owner had died.

Eachan huffed.

Hagano commanded the bear to stab the sword through the back of one of the frozen bears. It wouldn't kill the bear, nor cause it pain, which is exactly what Hagano wanted. This way he could stab Eachan while keeping him trapped.

The bear struggled to push the blade through its brother's frozen hide, but managed. Inch by inch, the blade plunged through the bear's gut until something stopped it.

Hagano had predicted that Eachan would keep his defenses up and stop the sword. But he had learned something valuable during the fight. Hagano had used two bears to move a frozen one—like a hammer and a nail. He could do the same now.

The bear beat its paws into the sword, causing it to plunge deeper into the mass of bears. The blade barely moved with each push, but little by little, made progress.

"Ecret knew we were coming," said Eachan. "And he did nothing about it."

The bear froze up with another jab at the sword.

Eachan thrust his knived-fingers out from his cage, sending the bear in front of him out of existence. He lunged at Hagano and thrust his gloves into Hagano's chest. The two tumbled to the ground. Eachan pinned his enemy down with little resistance.

Hagano kicked his legs and flailed what was left of his arms to no avail. The knives cut straight into Hagano's chest, but this time he was not trapped by Eachan's power. Every shred of pain stung like lightning in his lungs. His blood poured out of his wounds and onto Eachan's hand. His power tried to bring him relief, but could do nothing with the daggers still inside him. Hagano screamed. He summoned a bear, but it froze at Eachan's side.

Eachan's intentions were suddenly apparent. He wasn't going to freeze Hagano. He was going to keep his knives inside him to prevent him from healing. This was how he could die. Even if Eachan missed Hagano's heart, he could still bleed out. The sharp pains in his chest were like an echo of having his heart ripped out, but now the pain would not go away. Hagano squirmed weakly to try and break free, but without hands, he could do nothing.

"I tried to be merciful," Eachan whispered. He clawed away at Hagano's chest, ripping his skin and bones apart over and over as Hagano healed.

A burst of chickens snapped into being. They too fell prey to Eachan's freezing. Nothing helped. Hagano tried for an elephant, but failed. He told himself to make another bear. If he could only get it to bite Eachan's arm, then he might be able to break free. But all of his bears were detained. He already reached his limit. *Make a bear!* The command felt as if it would pull Hagano in two. What remained of his arms were on the verge of bursting. *Now!*

Hagano's left arm exploded. A spatter of blood, muscle, and bone flew into Eachan's face. Hagano screamed.

A seventh bear appeared and clenched its jaw onto Eachan's arm. Before tooth could pierce flesh, it too locked up. As did Hagano, relieving him of his pain. Both he and the bear froze simultaneously. Hagano commanded his arm to regrow, hoping that the tar in his arm left when it burst.

A buzz released Hagano from the freeze, but kept the bear locked up. The storm in his chest returned. At least, if nothing else, the bear prevented Eachan from moving that arm and ripping Hagano even more apart. The knives on that hand held still.

The gaping wound at Hagano's shoulder healed over at the joint. Something still kept him from fully healing. A swell of adrenaline kept him awake, but his strength was fading. He tried to heal his chest as best he could, but gained little ground with the knives still in inside him. Stretching his power gained him nothing. Trying that again would only do the same. His only thought was to make a crocodile. If he could place it between him and Eachan, he might be able to break free. But it wouldn't come. His chicken had fetched a piece of the crocodile-skinned drum, but he couldn't figure out why he couldn't make his power work. *What did I do wrong? What did I miss?*

Pieces in his mind locked into place. Click. Not all the drums were made of crocodile.

Hagano looked at the frozen bear trying to bite Eachan's arm. *Bite!* He commanded, but not the bear. Just as he hoped, a python appeared inside the bear's mouth and bit into Eachan's arm. For once, Eachan had not seen the attack coming.

Eachan pulled his hand out of Hagano's chest and through the bear's mouth with the python still latched onto his skin. The glove caught on the bear's teeth and slid off. Eachan froze the snake, but it didn't stop his bleeding. He screamed in pain and sliced away the serpent. Staggering, he pressed his injured arm to his chest.

Hagano rolled onto his side, trembling. He'd healed. The pain vanished, but the memory of it still had control over him.

Eachan put his mouth on the snake bite, then spat out the blood he had sucked.

Hagano's eyes widened. *He thinks it's venomous?* "That won't work." Hagano sat up. "Pythons have too much venom to be sucked out." A swarm of pythons materialized at Hagano's feet.

Panting and sweating, Eachan fled.

Hagano needed a moment to recover before he could chase him. He'd need his companions to unfreeze if he had any hope of continuing. One by one, a new flock of chickens appeared. He sent them away—following Eachan as he disappeared into the city streets.

Each bear unfroze in quick succession. The rope controlling the elephant buzzed and lost its rigid shape and fell to the ground. Fifteen seconds later, the elephant fell too. It landed on its side and struggled to stand with an injured leg. Hagano sent the bears to kill it. They clawed at its throat. It showed no signs of pain before vanishing.

One of the bears walked over to Hagano. It laid down on its stomach so he could climb on top and steady himself for a bumpy ride. Without hands, he wouldn't be able to stay on, let alone chase Eachan. Hagano called the pythons to him. The snakes slithered atop the bear, wrapped around Hagano's waist, his upper arm, and his legs. They constricted just enough to hold Hagano tight and then bit into the bear. It seemed strange, but managed to steady Hagano much more than he could himself.

The remaining five bears ran past Hagano at full speed. Clucking chickens sounded off in the distance, pointing the way to Eachan. The bears followed swiftly. At the end of the line, Hagano and his mount ran off too.

They charged through the streets. The bears sped past homes and through alleys, passing some of the chickens that pointed the way. It didn't take long for the bears to find Eachan. They stopped the moment he came into view.

Eachan panted heavily against a wall. Trapped in a corner, he had come to a dead end. He reached into a pouch and pulled out a handful of pebbles. Squeezing them, a buzz charged them with his power. Blood dripped down his arm. It pooled next to him. He panted heavily. A racing heart would only make his wounds bleed more steadily.

Hagano sent five of the bears charging. As predicted, Eachan threw his powered stones at each of them. In rapid succession, he threw them, immobilizing one and then missing another. He stopped four of them with the rocks and the final one with a fist.

Still riding a bear, Hagano raced towards Eachan. Without enough time to withdraw more stones, Eachan ripped the pouch off his belt and threw it at the bear upon which Hagano sat. It hit. The bear froze, but Hagano didn't. Caught in the momentum of the charge, the pythons' grip failed, sending Hagano flying over the bear and onto the stone streets. He landed flat on his back, knocking the air out of him.

"You don't want to kill me," Eachan said, a panic in his voice.

Hagano scrambled to his feet, still fighting for breath. He ran towards Eachan again. Just as soon as he got close enough, Hagano made a flurry of chickens fall in front of Eachan's face to block his view.

Backed against the wall, Eachan swiped the birds in front of his eyes. Just as soon as the chickens cleared, an elephant materialized before him. Its tusks shot out to either of his sides. They pierced through the wall with a booming crash. Just as the elephant's trunk slammed against Eachan's chest, it stopped in place, seized by Eachan's power. He found himself stuck between a wall, an elephant, and its tusks. He wriggled in place, unable to escape. Eachan screamed angrily. "Stop!"

An enormous sense of relief washed over Hagano. Was this it? Had he defeated his enemy? The man still drew breath, but no amount of writhing would free him. Hagano had won.

"You don't want to kill me."

"That's true. I don't want to." Hagano squinted. "But I think I have to."

"Please." Eachan strained for breath. "You don't understand what's truly happening."

"And you're going to tell me what is true? Why would I believe you?"

"Spare my life and Inturon will save you from The Sylph King."

Hagano stood back. "Yes. That's why he's here." His mind felt fuzzy—something was off. "What does that have to do with you?"

Eachan calmed. "My power comes from Inturon. Spare me and I will convince him to help you."

Shaking his head, Hagano stepped back. If Eachan's power came from Inturon, then the god was working with The Sylph King. It made no sense. Hagano held a memory of Inturon—one where he showed love to Ecret. He wouldn't backstab his brother just like Hagano would never betray Alessi. Whatever game Eachan was playing wasn't worth the time. Hagano needed to find Inturon and help him defeat The Sylph King.

"I will not kill you." Hagano bowed his head. "But I cannot let you roam free." He walked up to Eachan's side, but made sure to stay out of reach. "Can you use your power on yourself?"

"Yes." A worried look shot across Eachan's face.

"Then open your mouth."

"Why?" Eachan scowled.

"If you want to live, open your mouth," Hagano repeated.

Reluctantly, Eachan followed orders. A python appeared on his tongue. He cringed.

"Freeze yourself." Hagano told the snake to slither down his throat. Its tail hung from Eachan's mouth.

"Now freeze the snake."

Eachan did so.

Another python appeared and wrapped itself around Eachan's neck. It squeezed his throat before freezing in place. Another snake materialized, this one sitting on Hagano's shoulder. It locked eyes with Eachan, pulled back, and launched itself straight at Eachan's right eye. The moment its fang touched Eachan's eyeball, it stopped midair.

"One of three things will happen. One of your allies will come and save you or I will come and free you. In either of these cases, you live." Hagano looked into Eachan's visible eye. "Or you will try and escape, lose an eye, and die from the venom in your veins." Hagano almost felt sorry. This type of python wasn't venomous—he was sure of it. He always feared snakes and had spent a great deal of time learning about them in hopes of quelling the fear. It didn't work.

Now Hagano knew something Eachan didn't. There was nothing toxic in Eachan's veins, but it was crucial that he believed there was. A misconception about the snake bite was as good as actual venom. "Goodbye, Eachan."

The bears broke free of the time dilation. Hagano had them kill the elephant once more. With this fight over, Hagano once again climbed atop a bear and rode away.

CHAPTER TWENTY
INTO THE LION'S DEN

The mob of bears strolled down the streets back to the temple plaza. By some miracle Hagano made it this far. He needed to dwell on that fact, mostly because it kept out the thoughts that he would soon be walking into the most dangerous place in the world. He rested his head on his mount's back, nestling his ear between the bear's shoulders. It was warm and soft, even more so than the bearskin pelt from which it was made. Exhaustion sunk into him. It had been so long since he'd slept.

The parade of bears landed at the base of the temple plaza. Hagano sent one to claw away at the drums. Some of them were made of crocodile, he was sure of it—but he couldn't trace his confidence back to anything. Maybe he'd read about them at some point and filed the information away. Countless hours spent in the library had to be worth something.

He sat up on his mount and stared at the temple gates. The Sky Spear had crashed past the front doors. It left a gaping hole in the building and debris everywhere. So much of the steeple blocked the way to Ecret's hanging body that he couldn't reach it. The only way into the temple would be through the hole of the building the broken steeple created.

The bear returned and dropped a fragment of scaly skin from its mouth. The skin had no pattern, looking gray and dirty.

A chicken plucked it from the ground and delivered it to him. It tasted exactly how he anticipated—leathery, burnt, and covered in dirt. Without anything to wash it down, the skin scraped his throat.

Hagano never cared much for reptiles. Snakes in particular always frightened him. Most of his fear was irrational. He knew that. But snakes could be found easily, not in the dense parts of the city, but outside the city borders where Ecretian birds nested. As a child, he would go fishing with his father and watch them from a distance.

This is it. He cleared his throat. Despite racking his brain on where he would find more animals, he had nothing.

A breeze blew from the hole in the temple's side, creating an ominous howl. Clouds passed under the full moon, deepening the dark of night until moving on. Hagano had nothing left to do but test the limits of his power. Then off to the lion's den.

On his command, a python appeared next to him. He winced. Instinct told him to distance himself, but logic kept him in place. It posed no threat—he knew this. Fighting the voice that told him to run, he made the python slither up the bear and across his shoulders.

The weight of the serpent caught him off guard. It was much heavier than a chicken, which was the only thing he thought to compare it to. Not that chickens weighed much. The python stretched its body, proving longer than it seemed at first blush. If he were to guess, the snake could extend longer than Hagano's body.

It wrapped around Hagano's neck and chest, trying to find balance. Its cold scales were softer than expected. He'd anticipated hating the feel of it, but something about it calmed him. "Don't strangle me."

Pythons had no venom in their bite—a fact he never anticipated using as a weapon. His battle with Eachan would have ended much differently if Eachan had known that. But could he pull the same trick twice? Would the cheetah-faced woman have the same reaction?

The snake slithered back to the ground.

If the cheetah-faced woman was anything like the sylphs she

seemed to command, her blood was acid and would eat away the snake if it stuck its fangs into her. Hagano hoped that wasn't the case, but if it were, constricting might be an advantage. The snakes could strangle her without tapping into her blood.

Hagano reached out with the stub of his arm. A dozen pythons appeared. He pushed for more without counting them, but nothing happened. Either he wasn't being forceful enough or there were no more to be had. He chewed on his lip—he didn't want to know. Pushing his power too hard had made his arm explode. His shoulder healed over—but the memory of the pain was fresh. He rolled his shoulder joint, feeling it anew. No pain. He smiled. In some sense of poetry, his bad shoulder was the one that had burst. His power replaced it with a fully-functioning one. For the first time in months, it didn't hurt.

Hagano turned his attention to the crocodiles. One appeared, then a second. A third and fourth came, but a fifth didn't answer his call. He held back a sigh—hoping for more.

The crocodiles' gray skin hid them in the darkness. Their scales covered their entire bodies in what looked like armor. They stood like statues.

One elephant, seven bears, four crocodiles, fifty or so pythons, and countless chickens—this was everything. His eyes wandered up to the night sky. Would it be enough?

He shook his head. *It has to be.*

The jagged terrain of the temple steps seemed impossible for the crocodiles to navigate. The snakes could make their way through it, maybe. He shook his head. No reason to not unmake them and recreate them once inside.

The snakes offered their heads to the mouth of the crocs and the bears crushed the crocs in return. The serenity of the massacre gave Hagano chills. The creatures made no attempt to survive, nor did they react to their own destruction. They weren't wild, living animals. Their deaths defied the natural order. Hagano nodded. Sending empty shells to do his bidding was a thought much easier to swallow.

He took a deep breath and peered into the makeshift entrance to the temple. *Do or die.* Ecret's body needed to be pulled inside. His blood needed to be extracted from the cheetah-faced woman's tar. Inturon needed to be informed of the details of Ecret's demise. As far as Hagano knew, he was the only one left do all three.

Alessi. Hagano ground his teeth. Tears welled up in his eyes, but he fought them back. *Please be safe.*

"No sense in waiting," he mumbled. "You can do this." The pythons securing Hagano to the bear unhinged their jaws, releasing him. He slid off his mount. *Ecret put his faith in you for a reason... right?*

A sinking dread dropped from his throat to his stomach. His heart raced as he followed the bears to the temple entrance. No sound came from inside. He hoped the silence was a sign of something good. Anything else probably meant trouble. He sidled up along the wall and peeked inside. Moonlight from the holes in the ceiling offered the only illumination.

The bears entered first and fanned out.

Broken stone figures lay crumbled in every corner of the throne room. Limp bodies of guards, splattered by tar, dotted the floor. *Alessi?* Hagano's lip trembled.

He rushed from body to body, looking for his brother. Familiar faces, scarred by the tar, greeted him—but he couldn't remember their names. The meeting at the safe house felt like ages ago.

A rancid stench swelled up from the bodies and attacked his nose. He tilted his head, wishing he could ignore the rot that had built up over the past two days. Using a bear, he closed each guard's eyes as he went from one to the next. The first wasn't Alessi—he let go of the breath he was holding. But body after body passed, each a face of an ally. His anxiety grew at the sight of them. None so far were his brother, but he'd never stop worrying until he heard Alessi say he was okay.

The body of another guard caught his eye. It slumped over on its side at the far end of the room. Something about its shape made his chest hurt—something familiar. Dark, curly hair obscured the body's face. Hair like Hagano's. A tingling crept over his eyes, drying them in an instant. Tears swelled, but he pushed them back.

He ran up to whoever it was. Every part of him shook. His aching chest thumped up and down, taking shallow breaths. "Alessi?" he whispered. Peeking over the body, the familiar shape of Alessi's nose, his bushy eyebrows, his strong jaw, revealed the one person Hagano wished not to see.

Alessi didn't move. He didn't react. He did… nothing

"Alessi?" Hagano spoke up. His brother must have not heard him. The body stayed still.

"I came back." Hagano bit his lip to keep his teeth from chattering.

Tears streamed down his cheeks. Without his hands to clear them, they dripped down to his shirt. Everything felt hot. His head dizzied. The world blurred. "Alessi… please."

"Welcome home," boomed a voice from inside the chamber. The words filled Hagano with a familiar warmth—the same warmth Ecret's voice always brought. He turned around, convinced for a second that Ecret stood behind him.

The Sylph King sat on the hanging throne—a giant stalactite carved into a perch. "You'll have to forgive the mess. I just moved in."

The warmth gave way to a paralyzing chill. Hagano's body felt limp. His knees buckled, dropping him to the floor. Absolute dread, like liquid darkness, spread through his veins and numbed his bones.

The Sylph King pushed himself off from Ecret's hanging throne and glided to the center of the room. The bones and swords protruding from his body clanked together. He walked toward Hagano at a restrained pace.

Without thinking, Hagano scrambled to stand between his brother and The Sylph King. The seven bears turned to face the enemy. An elephant snapped into being beside them. A flood of snakes poured out of the air. *Go!*

All at once, the creatures attacked, stampeding towards the demon.

The Sylph King raised a hand and flicked his wrist. All of Hagano's animals flew across the room and vanished. "Where are your manners?"

Hagano's gut sank. His mouth dried. A flick of the wrist outweighed all of Hagano's powers—unmaking his army. "Leave." Hagano stepped toward The Sylph King. He did not know what compelled him to advance. He just knew he wasn't going to run. "This is not your temple."

"What a pious little creature you are." The sylph crept closer. "Tell me, are you not afraid?"

Was his fear that obvious? Wouldn't everyone be afraid? But Hagano refused to admit to it. "Ecret is on my side."

"Ecret was on their side too." The Sylph King waved a hand at the dead guards on the floor. "Don't tell me your faith still lies with the corpse hanging outside on the wall."

"He is still with me."

"Wrong." The Sylph King stopped in front of Hagano. His hunched back stretched upright, towering over him. "*I* am with you."

Hagano looked up into the shadowy cowl of The Sylph King. He couldn't see a face. Only darkness. "Where is Inturon?"

The Sylph King hissed a laugh. "Inturon? The endling? Don't tell me you'd abandon your god at the first sight of another. Where are your loyalties?"

Something made Hagano's mind feel fuzzy. Was it the fear? Adrenaline? A missing puzzle piece that would reveal his path forward? "Inturon and Ecret are on the same side."

A dark hand rested on Hagano's shoulder. It felt cold. "How misguided you are. Inturon and Ecret have not been on the same side for a very long time."

Hagano rolled his shoulder out from under The Sylph King's hand. "But they're brothers." *Brothers.* The word stung. He glanced back at Alessi's body.

"Would a true brother betray his kin?" The Sylph King started to pace.

Hagano played with his jaw. "What are you saying?"

"The gods are immortal, yet Ecret is dead." Metallic clunks sounded with the sylph's every step. "One might conclude that Ecret was no god at all and therefore, not Inturon's brother."

"I know he was." The back of Hagano's heel bumped something soft. He flinched, pulling his foot away from what he assumed was Alessi.

"I'm sure you do." The Sylph King nodded his head. "After all, you have a very special power." He waved a hand. "And the very special memory that comes with it."

The memory? Flashes of a young Inturon teaching Ecret at the pond burst into his mind. Hagano shook his head. "How do you know about that?"

"Dear boy." The sylph stopped. "There were two of us at the pond that day."

Us? The word screamed at him. *Us?* What did he mean? His thoughts felt stuck, tangled in a knot impossible to unravel.

The Sylph King reached across his chest, grabbed his shadowy cloak, and pulled it off. The rusted swords in his back dissipated into smoke. The bones and cloak vanished like candle-fire in the wind. All that was The Sylph King dispersed, leaving a different figure in his stead—a person, half-man and half-bearcat. This was the boy who taught Ecret how to use the same power Hagano now possessed. This was Inturon, grown into a full-fledged god.

CHAPTER TWENTY-ONE
COWED BY POWER

Inturon bore no resemblance to Ecret. He was part man, part mammal. His body was mostly human, as far as Hagano could tell. He wore long, baggy trousers, but no shirt. A round medallion hung among a string of beads around his neck. His arms changed from the skin of a man, to the fur of a bearcat. His head turned into that of an animal just above his mouth. A clear gem floated in the air above his brow.

The sight of The Sylph King stripping away his cloak to reveal Inturon underneath blanked Hagano's mind. Was this some sort of illusion created by The Sylph King? Or was it truly Inturon who had disguised himself as Ecret's nemesis? But why?

"You look confused." Inturon waved a paw. His cat-like ear flicked.

The ground under Hagano moved, forming itself into a chair.

Inturon nudged Hagano into it. "Let me clear things up for you. I've come to liberate you."

"Liberate me?" Hagano's whole body stiffened.

"There is no Sylph King. Never was." The light caught the gem floating in front of Inturon's brow. It glimmered white. "My brother was a liar, down to the bone. He deceived you. He deceived millions."

Inturon waved his hand and made a seat for himself across from Hagano. "He even deceived me."

Ecret's words repeated in Hagano's head. *Lies and deceit are weapons we use against our enemies, not our friends.* If Inturon was The Sylph King, then he was an enemy, which meant he would not be telling the truth.

"What is your name, boy?"

He wanted to keep silent, but fear compelled him to answer. "Hagano."

"Tell me Hagano." Inturon eased into his seat. "Your god is dead. Loyalty to him and his lies will no longer serve you. I, however, am still very much a god." He grinned. "So tell me, where is the endling?"

"The endling?" Hagano scrunched his face. Inturon's words swam in his head. Ecret wasn't a liar. The Sylph King was real. How did Ecret deceive his brother? Was Inturon not the endling?

"Yes." Impatience filled Inturon's tone. "Earn your place in my new kingdom. Lead me to the endling."

Hagano shook his head. "You are the endling."

"Don't play dumb." Inturon folded his legs and placed his paws on his knees. "Anyone with your power would know Ecret's secrets." His ears flicked.

The thumping of Hagano's heart pulsed in his ears. *Say something.* But what? None of this made sense. Should he pretend to know? Could he leverage Inturon's false belief? Why was Ecret's brother antagonizing him?

"You defy me." Inturon sat back. "Intellect like roaches. Don't you understand? There is no paradise. There is no Sylph King. And there is no Ecret." Inturon's lips pulled back, revealing sharp canines.

Closing his eyes, Hagano tried to focus on his thoughts. Ecret never taught that the other gods were malicious, but Inturon seemed to be acting out of revenge. Something wasn't adding up. "I don't believe you."

Inturon rested his head against his fist. "If it is proof you need to obey my commands, then so be it."

"Proof?"

"Did Ecret teach you that gods are immortal?" Inturon rose to his feet.

Hagano nodded.

"I am a god. Test Ecret's teachings. Try and kill me."

This was a trap – it had to be a trap. *What do I do?* Hagano's heart and mind reached out to Ecret. *Tell me what to do.*

No answer came. Of all the moments to feel abandoned by Ecret, why did it have to be this one?

"Go on." Inturon crossed his legs and laid back into his seat. "Here, use this." Inturon turned his head to look behind him.

At the far end of the room, a sword flew off the ground, shot through the air like an arrow, and stabbed into Hagano's chair, barely missing his ear.

Hagano gasped. His eyes glanced at the sword, then down at the short ends of his arms. He couldn't wield a sword—that should be obvious to Inturon. What was he trying to do?

"Obedience isn't without its rewards." Inturon walked up to Hagano. He placed his paws on the stub of Hagano's arm and shoulder. "Foreign blood clings to your muscles. Its strength and your power are equally matched, keeping you from healing. Let me clear it."

The ends of Hagano's arms burned. The pain sharpened, like hot daggers cutting into his bones. He clenched his teeth, squelching the cries that rose in his throat.

Black acid melted through the pores on Hagano's arms. It dripped out of his skin and onto Inturon's paws. The god looked undisturbed by the tar. He tossed it to the ground.

"Go ahead." The god nodded at Hagano before settling back into his chair.

Heal. The command awakened Hagano's power. A tingling spread from his mouth, down his neck, into his shoulders, reaching the ends of his arms. They grew, forming elbows, then forearms, wrists, and hands. Skin wrapped around muscle as it wrapped around bones.

The weight of Hagano's wounds vanished. His body felt light. His arms looked pristine, completely unblemished. He crossed his arms and rubbed his fingers on his newfound flesh. It felt like a silky balm. He wanted to smile, but the sight of them scared him. The memory of a young Inturon came to mind. He felt an immense gratitude then. He felt it again now.

Inturon's words repeated in Hagano's mind. *There is no Sylph King.*

But why would Inturon masquerade as Ecret's enemy? Could it be possible—*No. Don't think it....* Was Inturon telling the truth? Ecret lied. Everything Hagano believed was fake. There was no paradise.

Inturon's finger twitched. The sword offered itself to Hagano. "Go on. Take it. Try to slay me."

The melody of Inturon's words filled Hagano's chest with a warmth that gave him strength. The peace that surrounded the god scared him. It felt too familiar. If he closed his eyes, he might have thought he was sitting in the company of his own god.

"Take the sword. End me."

Hagano reached out and took hold of the hilt. Not wanting to move, he averted his eyes, looking at anything but the god. He wished he could shrink into the darkness of the room and escape Inturon's gaze. It bore into him.

"You test my patience, Hagano."

Hagano pointed the sword at Inturon's chest and took a deep breath.

"Don't be so half-hearted." An unseen force pulled the sword up. Inturon opened his mouth and waved the sword into it with a paw. The god peered into Hagano's eyes and gave a slight nod.

Hagano couldn't move. He didn't know if he should actually listen to Inturon and try and stab him or if it would be better to not try at all. He had fallen into some sort of mind game. *What good it would do to try and stab a god? But disobeying him can't end well either.*

Gritting his teeth, Hagano tightened his grip on the hilt. His sweaty palm made it difficult to hold. He took another deep breath, then lunged forward. He knew the god wouldn't let himself be killed, but Hagano didn't anticipate trying to stab a mountain. The collision swept the blade from his hand and sent him stumbling. The sword clanged as it hit the floor.

"See? Immortal." Inturon motioned back to the chair sitting across from him.

Hagano took the cue and sat back down.

"Gods are immortal, Hagano. It is our nature." Inturon leaned forward. "Ecret is dead. Therefore, not a god."

"Was he ever?" Hagano couldn't believe he was entertaining the idea—but it all clicked together in his mind. It made sense. It hurt, but it did make sense.

"Yes, originally." Inturon bowed his head. "But no longer. Ecret has sinned."

"Sinned?"

The god looked pleased by the question. "There is but one way for a god to lose his immortality." Inturon paused. His cat-like ear flicked. "Those of us who live outside of death cannot interfere with its affairs. But if one steals from death, then death demands payment."

"What are you saying?" Hagano stared at his feet.

"Ecret willfully and directly took a life." A soft chuckle entered the end of the sentence. "He's a murderer."

Murderer? A numbness welled up within Hagano. It pulled him down. Everything turned heavy. His arms, his head, his chest. He didn't want to believe Inturon. He knew he shouldn't, but he did. Ecret was dead when he should have been immortal. The only explanation he had was the one Inturon offered and it was far worse than Hagano could have imagined. Ecret was a murderer. And a liar. And not a god.

"Now tell me." Inturon shifted in his seat. "Where is the endling?"

Hagano tensed. He fidgeted in his seat. "I..."

A low growl rumbled under Inturon's breath. "I heal you. I speak truth to you. I prove my divinity." He pounded a fist against the arm of his seat. "Yet you still deny me."

Beads of cold sweat ran down Hagano's neck. Words escaped him.

"Have you no fear of death?" Inturon's words neared hissing.

Click. Wandering thoughts connected in Hagano's mind. He met Inturon's gaze. "You cannot kill me." Then he would have sinned and lose his immortality—like Ecret.

The god's eyes narrowed. "So feckless are the young." He gripped the beads around his neck and thumbed them one by one. "Show me the extent of your power."

Hagano blanched. He dared not refuse. Closing his eyes, he created everything he could. An elephant, pythons, crocodiles, rabbits, and chickens spread across the room. The bears near Alessi's body joined him at his side.

"Let me offer you some perspective." Inturon's gem glowed white. "You have shown me seven bears. I will show you seventy." Bear after bear materialized around him, crushing the snakes and chickens at their feet. Hagano commanded them to distance themselves. "You've made a hundred snakes. I give you a thousand." Waves of pythons poured into the room.

Hagano's eyes watered. Inturon's display of power stole more and more of his hope with each passing moment. Glancing around the room, Hagano's army was lost in a sea of the enemy's forces. He focused his mind on one thought and sent rabbits and chickens out the front gate.

"I would make a hundred elephants, but the room is starting to feel cramped." The light in Inturon's gem faded. "Now imagine the wide variety of creatures I could make that you cannot." The god flicked his ears. "There is no point in resisting."

Hagano looked at the ground behind him. Only Alessi's messy hair was visible from where he sat. His heart sunk. Alessi was dead. The fact choked his throat and strangled his chest. Inturon gloated over the fact that he was still immortal—because unlike Ecret, he had not killed. But he had. He killed Alessi. No reward, no threat, no truth could compel Hagano to deal with the one who murdered his brother.

Lies and deceit are weapons we use against our enemies.

Hagano looked into Inturon's eyes. "I will take you to the endling."

The god tilted his head. "At long last, reason prevails." He clapped his paws together and called out into the room. "Madigan."

The cheetah-faced woman appeared out of the shadows, a handful of men in her wake.

The sight of her did not frighten Hagano like it had before. She was another enemy, but the exact one he needed.

Madigan's crew waded through the sea of animal life until they reached Inturon. She knelt at the god's side and uttered something in a language Hagano didn't understand—Inturoni, he assumed.

Why aren't they back yet? Hagano eyed the door. He needed more time for the rabbits to return.

"Lead the way." Inturon stood.

"Tell me one thing first." Hagano cleared his throat.

Madigan scoffed, seemingly insulted by Hagano's refusal to follow Inturon's every whim.

"Yes?" Inturon's look sharpened into a scowl.

Hagano interlocked his fingers and squeezed. "You said Ecret deceived you. How?" He hoped the story would be long—at least long enough.

Cocking his head, Inturon ran his tongue over his teeth. "Before Ecret isolated himself inside his barrier mountains, we were allies. His forces and mine fought the other gods, but Ecret began to think the endless wars did nothing but hurt you meaningless humans." He flashed his teeth. "He tried to convince me to join him in isolation, but I refused. So he played along in our war games, tricking me into thinking he would always be my ally, until the day came when he lead an exodus into these lands and cut himself off from the rest of the world... leaving me outnumbered. And weak."

Hagano nodded. "You hate him."

A deep shade of red flushed Inturon's cheeks. "There is nothing in this world I hate more than my brother."

A rabbit hopped onto Hagano's lap. *Finally.*

Hagano held his hand under its mouth and looked up to Inturon. "I feel sorry for you."

Inturon straightened his back and clenched his paws.

Madigan tensed, watching Inturon as if he would signal her to attack.

The gem at Inturon's brow turned black.

Hagano nodded. "I have a lot of questions."

"I have answered enough of your questions!" Inturon crouched as if to strike.

Sitting back, Hagano let in a cool breath. "My questions aren't for you."

The rabbit dropped a piece of flesh from its mouth into Hagano's hand. He threw it between his teeth and swallowed.

A surge of energy filled Hagano, making his bones feel as if they'd burst into a thousand pieces. His new arms melted away. His chest burned hotter than fire, igniting his shirt. The energy pulled Hagano to his feet. An agonizing scream bellowed from his stomach.

Chickens poured out from his arms and chest, then vanished into wisps of steam. Bears followed, as did pieces of human arms. His screams echoed throughout the chamber. A python slithered out of his mouth, muffling the sound of his pain. Crocodiles, rabbits, and horrible amalgamations of beasts and man erupted from him. They materialized and disappeared all in an instant.

Madigan stood back. Inturon stared at Hagano as the shifting bodies cascaded from him.

Beast after beast drained out of Hagano's arms and chest. He coughed up more pythons, dulling his screams. The rush of creatures extinguished the fire on his chest. He struggled to breathe as more serpents filled his mouth.

Hagano's arms turned to talons. They stretched out, extending into full legs. Ecret's head burst through Hagano's chest, his horns tearing through Hagano's skin like knives. Ecret's neck reached out, followed by his torso and wings. His body connected with the legs that protruded from Hagano's arms. Hagano fell back into the chair as Ecret fully formed in front of him. Just as the entirety of his god emerged, Hagano's chest and arms reformed into their natural state.

Ecret flapped his wings sharply. A myriad of ethereal spears flew throughout the room, killing every one of the creatures Inturon summoned. They all burst into nothingness. One set of spears pierced Madigan and her men, knocking each of them to the ground with holes in their chests.

"Hello brother," Ecret said, staring straight into Inturon's disbelieving eyes.

CHAPTER TWENTY-TWO

FLESH AND BLOOD

"What a sad state you find yourself in." Inturon eyed Ecret's new body. "That form looks like it will fall apart at any moment." He jumped backward, flying in the air and sitting back down on Ecret's hanging throne.

Leaning over to Hagano, Ecret spoke softly, "You've done well." He lifted a talon and gently tapped Hagano's brow.

"What are you doing?" Hagano went crossed-eyed trying to see his own forehead.

"Marking you."

A cold stream of liquid swirled on Hagano's skin, forming what he assumed was Ecret's crest—a small image of the avian god.

Ecret pulled back his talon. "When this mark burns, make me a new body." He flew through the air and crashed into the ceiling, breaking off giant pieces of stone.

They smashed against the ground, crushing Madigan and her attendants as they struggled to remove the ethereal spears pinning them to the floor.

Hagano covered his eyes with an arm as a wave of dust flew through the room.

The cloud passed. Hagano looked to Ecret, who clung to what remained of the temple walls. Ecret's eyes pointed to the hanging throne, where Madigan now sat hunched over.

Did they switch?

Inturon burst through the rocks that should have crushed Madigan.

Lowell's switching power. Hagano cringed. If Inturon had Lowell's power again, then what Jaga said was correct—powers return to a god after the human host dies. And this power was difficult enough to deal with when only Jaga was fighting. Hagano couldn't hide behind a bookcase this time.

A strange splat sounded from the direction of the throne.

Madigan's muculent body slid out of the throne and onto the floor. The hole in her body formed by the spear filled with tar. It rippled over her as it reassembled her bones and muscles—a grotesque and seemingly painful version of Hagano's ability to heal.

Reaching out, Hagano sicced his bears on her. Their massive bodies rumbled with every step. But before they neared her, their paws lifted off the ground. Floating mid-air, they pedaled their paws, unable to kick their way to their target.

What's happening? Hagano looked around for an explanation.

Inturon jumped out from the stone pile. Staring straight at Hagano, he crouched and plunged a paw into the floor. A stream of energy erupted from his paw and beelined for Hagano. It shot through the floor and encircled him. Just as the ring of energy fully surrounded Hagano, the ground broke apart. Walls lifted themselves out of the floor, trapping him inside a stone cage.

Total darkness surrounded him. He put his hands out, feeling for a wall and punched the first one to come into reach. A solid stone block hit his knuckles and offered no give. He pushed against it, but nothing budged. He grunted. His bears were outside of the stone trap, so they couldn't help. None of the other animals had the strength, save an elephant, but he doubted there was room for one. He cursed himself for not keeping a bear at his disposal. That was a mistake he already made during his fight with Eachan. Was he not learning?

"Ecret!" he yelled, spinning around.

As happy as he was to bring back his god, the duplicate body Hagano gave him was not exactly the one Ecret wanted. It might not even be the one he needed to be restored to full strength. And here he was, once again, helpless.

With no way to engage, he tried to focus on the puzzle of the room and all its pieces—Ecret, Inturon, Madigan, himself. How could he maneuver everyone in a way that spelled victory? He chewed on his lip. Was it a puzzle to solve or a game to be won? Inturon had mentioned 'war games'. What did all this mean to him?

His guard training replayed in his mind. *The enemy will never tell you his weakness, but he will show it to you.* Alessi—those were his words. A sharpness squeezed his chest. He shook his head. He didn't have time to mourn. Alessi wouldn't want him to fail... or die. But had Inturon revealed his weakness?

What had Hagano learned already?

The bearcat god protected Madigan when Ecret attacked. He also trapped Hagano instead of trying to kill him. Inturon couldn't kill Hagano without 'sinning' and losing his immortality. Any move the god made against someone wouldn't be lethal. But how did it all work? Clearly the gods played a part in the deaths of thousands—especially if they went to war.

Madigan. Hagano. Divine powers. Click. Click. Click. The pieces linked together in his mind and his gut told him he'd found something. People could kill each other *for* the gods. That's how they fought while preserving their immortality. That's why Inturon protected Madigan. That's why she was the one at the first attack.

Click. Another piece found its place. Ecret had already lost his immortality. He could kill Madigan without losing anything.

Hagano balled his fists. This was their advantage. Ecret and Hagano could both end Madigan and reclaim Ecret's blood, but only Madigan could kill Hagano. Inturon would interfere, but never make a decisive blow. He probably wouldn't do anything to even risk it. No—the bear-cat god prided himself too much on his godhood.

Kill Madigan and the fight is over.

Click. Another thought landed—stripping away what hope built up inside Hagano. Inturon could not be killed. Ecret could. If Ecret died again, Madigan and Inturon would easily pick off Hagano.

The mark! The possibility of Ecret dying was the exact reason Ecret put the mark on Hagano's forehead. He knew his duplicate body was weak and would need replacing. Hagano would simply need to keep making more until they won.

The mark on Hagano's forehead sizzled in a fiery flash. Ecret had been killed, again. Hagano willed another body into the dark room. A thud sounded, making him think that a lifeless shell of the winged god slumped onto the ground. Unlike before, it didn't emerge from Hagano's chest and arms, but appeared just as every other animal.

"Lord?" Hagano whispered. Long seconds passed before there was any sign that the body surged to life. Then noise and a familiar voice.

"Again, well done," whispered Ecret. "We now have a moment before Inturon realizes that I am returned to life."

"I think I know what we need to do," Hagano said. "I kill Madigan and free your blood from her control. You distract Inturon."

Ecret shuffled in the darkness. "Precisely. I see why you have survived this long."

The compliment warmed Hagano's chest.

"Are you ready?"

"Yes." Hagano nodded, forgetting that Ecret couldn't see him.

The god stretched his wings, sending the stone walls flying outward. He waved one wing towards the floating bears, vaporizing them with more spears. With the other wing, he organized a swarm of stone spiders, identical to the ones that appeared at the festival.

Half the swarm scuttled toward Inturon while the rest scurried to Madigan—whose ebony sludge had made her whole.

Inturon stomped a foot. A shockwave tore through the stone creatures nearing him.

A hole broke open under Madigan's feet. She disappeared into it and the hole clammed shut. The rocky swarm reached where she had stood, then meandered about, unsure of where to find her.

She reappeared, rising through the floor next to the bodies of her dead attendants. The spears that pierced them punched through their hearts, leaving them to dissolve in their collective blood. As Madigan rose, the tar sizzled and boiled—excited by her presence.

She stepped to the center of the black pool, unconcerned by the acidic tar that ate away her shoes. Withdrawing a knife, she turned to face Hagano, her eyes fixating on him. In one swift move, she stabbed herself in the heart. A pained expression crossed her face, but was quickly replaced by a menacing smirk. Tar oozed out of her chest and down her legs. She withdrew the dagger, which was nothing more than the hilt, and cast it aside.

Kneeling among her fallen attendants, her blood mixed with theirs. The pool of tar livened. It reeked of burning flesh. The scent grew stronger as the blood swirled and boiled. The tar engulfed the remnants of the attendants' bodies. As soon as they vanished under the acid, a slew of black, dead hands shot out from the tar. They climbed Madigan's legs, eating her clothes until they covered everything but her eyes and mouth.

More human shapes clawed their way out of the pool. Their stringy frames struggled to stand. Webs of tar connected Madigan and these new monstrosities. She stood among her six tar puppets. Their shapes, while human-like, morphed and transformed with every passing second.

Hagano waved a hand, sending a new crop of beasts towards the horror that was now Madigan. Three crocodiles and a pair of bears ran at her. He held back the rest, not wanting to be trapped again without something he could call to his aid. Before the beasts reached her, an array of spears rained down towards Madigan, but shattered into harmless pieces before doing any damage.

It seemed Ecret had made an attack. And Inturon thwarted it.

Hagano was so focused on Madigan that he had stopped watching the two gods duel. That didn't matter. He needed to focus on his own fight. The gods bounded around the room, rocking it with thunderous clashes. The glimpses he caught of their battle made him understand why Eachan was sent to help kill Ecret. The god needed to be slowed if he were to be defeated.

The bears reached Madigan first. The six muculent puppets stretched their strings away from Madigan to meet them. Their arms sharpened into needles and sliced through the bears despite the puppets' frailty.

One bear pushed past the puppets and swiped its paw at Madigan.

She swatted the paw away, effortlessly dissolving it as it came into contact with her own tarry hand. The crocodiles arrived, biting at the enemy as soon as they could. They fared worse than the bears, popping out of existence as soon as their skulls were met with the puppets' strikes.

Hagano couldn't think of anything more to do but try and over-whelm Madigan with his beasts. Collectively, their assault might make a little progress. But he didn't have the luxury of time.

The mass of stringy puppets sprinted towards Hagano. Their mouths gaped open, shrieking an inhuman war cry. Madigan charged. Her footprints left sizzling black imprints on the stone floor. Reaching out her arm, Madigan sent the front most puppet up into the air and speeding its way on top of Hagano.

Leaping clumsily out of the way, Hagano managed to escape the bombing puppet's strike. He had little time to recover as Madigan kept sprinting towards him. Before he could think of a counterattack, the avian mark on his forehead burned. Hagano reached out his arms, making another body for Ecret.

The god instantly filled his new vessel and wasted no time orienting to a new location. He sunk the floor underneath Madigan and her minions, sending them into a pit deep enough that they could not climb out. A wave of stone creatures flung themselves into the pit, burying Madigan and all else inside it.

"Go!" Ecret screamed at Hagano, pointing a wing towards the door where his real body hung.

A mist of darkness shrouded the room, blocking out every trace of light. It covered the holes in the ceiling and the walls, blotting out the sky and masking all exits.

Pounding footsteps shook the ground. Hagano couldn't see the doorway anymore, but ran towards where he remembered it to be. It only took a few steps before he tripped on a piece of rubble and nearly fell. Behind him, an array of white lights scattered across the room. Dim at first, they illuminated everything as if he were standing in the middle of the night sky. He made a bear and climbed on top of it, thankful for his hands, then headed off again towards the exit and Ecret's real body.

Fresh night air greeted Hagano as a tangle of vines shot out from the floor, ensnaring him and his mount. They wrapped around his limbs and lifted both he and the bear into the air. The vines tightened, struggling against Hagano's writhing.

Two bears snapped into being and furiously went to work tearing up the vines. One freed Hagano's legs, but another vine whipped around them. More bears appeared, but they failed to free their maker as vines sprouted from every direction.

"I see what you're after." Inturon's voice vibrated through the room. The god threw his arm towards the wall above the main doors. A rope shot out from his paw and broke through the wall. Wrapping the end of the rope around his paw, Inturon jerked it back. Ecret's real body broke through the wall. It flew across the room and landed in the pit entombing the cheetah-faced woman. "Destroy it, Madigan!"

Coils of tar sprang up from the pit and wrapped around Ecret's real body—eating away its feathers and flesh.

Ecret sped towards it. Stone scorpions rained from the ceiling atop Madigan. They clawed away at her tar in an effort to free the body, but their pincers fell victim to the acid.

A storm of spears shot out from Ecret toward the sludge.

Inturon flew in front of them, ending their path. He flicked his tail. A stalactite broke from the ceiling. It pierced Ecret, unmaking his body.

Hagano's mark ignited. He summoned another Ecret. Vines

wrapped around him, but a storm of spears cut them down, freeing Ecret, Hagano, and the bears.

The bears plopped to the ground. One broke Hagano's fall.

Madigan's tar ravished the last of the real Ecret's body. Bones of the god, still intact, fell into the pit.

Hagano looked to Ecret.

He didn't move. Whatever hope they had of restoring Ecret vanished.

Failure—through and through. Hagano's jaw went slack. His eyes stayed glued to his god, but Ecret's expression offered no hint of his emotions. Was he in shock?

"Shame." Inturon gave a mocking frown. "I was hoping to keep your corpse, start a collection." The bearcat god strutted towards the pit. He glanced down at Ecret's bones. "Look at you, brother, dead inside a grave of your own making. How poetic."

"What now?" Hagano pulled his arm to his ribs as if his shoulder was still healing. For months the feel of his arm against his side brought him comfort, but now it felt pointless. Everything he did was to bring Ecret's blood back to a body that no longer existed. Based on Ecret's silence, Hagano guessed that even he didn't know how to proceed.

"There is but one outcome to this conflict." Inturon called out. "You die."

Madigan reformed her human shape behind the god. Her puppets returned to form their skeletal battalion.

Ecret kept his eyes on his brother, but lowered his voice so only Hagano could hear. "Create as many copies of me as you can." He stretched a wing. Stone creatures scuttled out of the ground and raced to Inturon.

Hagano wiped his sweaty palms against his pants. "But won't all the bodies be lifeless?" Ecret's soul would only be able to occupy one at a time.

"Trust me." Ecret's voice buzzed inside Hagano's chest.

Hagano made two copies of Ecret. As predicted, they slumped to the floor motionless. He pushed himself to make a third, fourth, and fifth. All came surprisingly easy. He created a sixth, but a seventh was his last. Including the body Ecret's spirit already occupied, that made eight. It felt like more than he should've been able to make. Ecret stood taller than a bear, of which Hagano's power could only make seven. The only explanation was that his power had grown somehow… possibly from eating Ecret's flesh.

Ecret swiped his wings over each of the copies, leaving his sigil on each of their faces. One by one, they sprang to life. Whatever Ecret's plan was, it seemed he would be hiding himself among decoys. The god swiped a wing across his own face, giving himself an identical mark.

"This isn't over, Hagano," one of the Ecrets said. "The plan remains. Kill Madigan. Now take these." Another one of the bird gods stretched its wings towards the pit that kept Ecret's bones. They rose into the air and flew towards the Ecret that called them.

Floating in the air, surrounded by several copies of Ecret, the two femur bones stretched and sharpened, transforming into swords.

Hagano reached out and took one in each hand. They were exceedingly long, but swinging them around was as easy as swinging a ribbon. Their lightness seemed like weakness, but Ecret wouldn't arm Hagano with something useless. Madigan had failed to even scratch them. The tar had no effect on the god's marrow.

One of the Ecrets stomped a talon. A hole opened up in the floor. A sealed wooden chest shot out of it and dropped in front of Hagano.

"What's this?" Hagano crouched in front of it.

"Something helpful, I hope." One of the Ecrets responded.

Inturon fell from above and smashed the chest. He spun around, hitting several Ecret bodies and sending them flying. His tail whipped Hagano's hands, knocking the swords to the ground. A slew of jars fell out of the chest and broke.

"Keep fighting," shouted Ecret. "I'll be back." The eight Ecret's flew away in different directions. Half disappeared down the temple hallways. The others went outside, flying away into the night.

Inturon's eyes darted around the room, tracking each version of his brother. A flock of hawks snapped into being in the air circling him. They split up, chasing each of the duplicate Ecrets. Inturon shouted something at Madigan and chased after one of the gods flying out into the city.

The darkness that filled the room dissipated. The glowing beads of lights remained, dangling in the room like stars.

One of the jars from the chest rolled closer to Hagano. It looked old and dusty, untouched for who knows how long. The dust flew into a puff as Hagano blew it away. The words 'Vervet Monkey' were painted onto it. Click—he knew what the chest contained. It was a cache of animal flesh.

The viscous tar skeletons shrieked. Madigan reached out her hands, making the puppets twitch. They charged.

Hagano sent up a wall of bears and crocodiles. He lunged at the chest, hoping to reach a few more jars before his defenses failed and he would have to flee. He grabbed the only jar he could reach as one of the puppets broke through the bears.

The puppet's body ate through the beast. It flopped onto the chest. The wood, the jars, and the flesh inside them dissolved in the black acid.

Hagano sprang to his feet and fled. As he ran, he looked at the only other jar he managed to save. It too had an inscription—Python. He groaned and tossed the jar, angry that he somehow grabbed one of the few animals already at his disposal. The monkey jar opened with a forceful twist. He emptied its contents into his hand and threw the small chunk of meat down his throat. It tasted fresh—seasoned even—strangely delicious for something in storage, even through a hint of burnt taste.

Five puppets kept on Hagano's tail.

Madigan stayed behind, controlling the strings of tar that connected her and her warriors. The murky attendants shrieked like pained animals. They flung bits of themselves at Hagano. The muddy clumps rained down around the room, burning everything that touched them.

Hagano summoned another wall of bears behind him and

commanded them to attack. He turned around and followed closely after.

A spray of tar hit the bears, but failed to kill them. The beasts continued full speed, unfazed by their sizzling wounds.

Hagano grunted, mad at himself. He'd left the bone swords with the broken chest. One of the tar fighters stood there, crouched over, trying to pick them up. The sword fell through its grip and landed back on the ground. Ecret's bones could not be harmed by the tar and seemingly, couldn't be handled by it either.

A dozen monkeys materialized around Hagano. Their black faces stood out from the fringe of white hair around them. Their bodies were mostly gray and stood two feet tall. They were no beasts of war, but at least they had thumbs. With any luck, they would be able to snatch the bone swords and bring them back to Hagano.

The monkeys darted off. They weaved past the bears and the puppets, reaching the swords and the tar figure that stood with them.

The black skeleton stopped trying to retrieve the sword and stood to defend it. The monkeys acted quickly, surrounding the creature, distracting it from one side while moving in from the other. With a few coordinated movements, they snatched the swords. Two of the monkeys carried away the swords, holding it with both hands. The sight was almost laughable—tiny monkeys carrying swords as tall as a man.

The animals darted back to Hagano's side. He took the swords from them, ready to fight and pleased with how useful the monkeys turned out to be.

The puppets leapt through the air. Hagano dispelled one with a single swipe and looked at the unharmed blade. *Better than steel.* He swung again, slicing its puppet strings.

The last string of tar disconnected from Madigan. The puppet lost its shape and melted into a puddle of ooze.

Hagano hopped in the air, putting a crocodile underneath him to avoid the tarry pool. Charging puppets clashed with frenzied bears. Just as soon as one disappeared, Hagano made another.

The puppets collected their fallen comrades and reattached their master's strings with a mere touch. Neither side seemed to be making any ground. Her tarry blood and his power, as Inturon put it, were equally matched.

A swirl of flesh formed an elephant at Hagano's side. It bowed its head and, with its trunk, helped Hagano climb onto its neck. Hagano held out his swords on each side, wielding what now looked like a second pair of tusks.

The elephant sped off towards Madigan, leaving the bears to battle the tar fighters.

Madigan poised herself to fight.

The mass of puppets shrieked again. They fled their fight against the bears and chased after the elephant. They moved swiftly, almost instantly catching up to the mammoth. Their muddy hands clawed at the beast with every step. Failing to slow it, they jumped onto its hide. Their touch burned away its flesh as they crawled over it.

Hagano cut them to pieces with the bone swords, knocking them off the elephant and severing their bond to their master.

The charging elephant neared Madigan.

The slime covering most of her body shifted around to mask her face. Pitch-black, she ran at the elephant. They collided head on. Her tarry armor seared through the beast's head, chest, and body.

The elephant vanished. Madigan showed no signs of damage.

Hagano fell to the floor. He rolled over the ground and back onto his feet.

Madigan turned to face him.

He held out the swords, knowing they were the only things that could stop the extreme power of the tar.

Madigan's forces collected at her side.

Hagano dashed at his opponent. Bears appeared, sped in front of him, and rampaged into the crowd of puppets. He neared Madigan and placed a bear on all fours in front of him. Hagano jumped off its back, placed a standing bear and leapt off of that one too. He jumped over Madigan and summoned another elephant and a slew of ten bears to fall onto his opponent.

Madigan's armor burnt through the thick of the beasts, but the amount of flesh was too great to vanish in an instant. She swung her arms around in the flood of creatures. Her hands crossed Hagano's legs, melting through them and severing his feet.

Hagano landed on a bear, doubling over as the pain of the tar ate away at him. The swords fell out of reach. *Heal!* His legs didn't. A pack of monkeys appeared next to him.

They took the swords and rushed to fight Madigan and her army. Each of the small creatures leapt around, spinning, throwing the swords back and forth, slicing the attendants, and keeping them busy.

The tar on his legs kept Hagano from regenerating. There was more corruption. The burning pain was all too familiar.

Hagano rolled off the bear and summoned a crocodile that chomped down on the ends of his legs. Its powerful jaw ripped off what Hagano assumed was the corrupted flesh, letting him regrow his legs and feet. He exhaled. The pain was gone.

Swift and nimble, the monkeys swept the blades through Madigan's body like fire through paper. They spun around, almost dancing as they sliced every black limb that dared draw close before swiping across Madigan's chest, cutting her in two.

She disintegrated into a pool of tarry blood.

The room fell silent.

The puppets and Madigan melted into nothing. The tar bubbled, but didn't remake Madigan's body.

Is this it? Hagano panted heavily. His eyes searched the tar for any sign of human shape.

Nothing.

Two Ecrets returned from outside. One flew straight to the ceiling. The other landed near Hagano.

"You're back." Hagano held a hand to his chest.

The clashing of metal echoed through the halls of the temple. Three Ecrets appeared, each from different hallways and each of them followed by a river of metal. Weapons, relics, armor, instruments, and every imaginable metallic object followed the duplicate gods into the room. The Ecrets flew around the chamber, pulling in wave after wave of items until the ceiling of the massive throne room was completely covered.

The Ecrets at the ceiling swirled around in the air, transforming the metallic objects into a floating river of water.

Hagano's heart sank. If Ecret could turn metal into water, then Jaga's power had returned to him. But that would only happen if...

Hagano covered his mouth with a trembling hand. *Jaga's dead?*

CHAPTER TWENTY-THREE
REPRISE

Madigan, the cheetah-faced woman, and her puppets were nothing more than a bog of acidic tar. Three Ecrets flew around the ceiling underneath the floating lake that just seconds ago had been made of metal. Hagano squeezed the bone swords in his hands. "Jaga?" Was he right—did Jaga die and give her power back to Ecret?

Jaga's not dead. Ecret's voice filled Hagano's mind, warming him with his usual soothing voice. *Trust me.*

The puddle of bubbling black sludge swirled.

Madigan isn't dead either.

Water droplets leaked from the floating lake at the top of the throne room. Ecret's power kept it suspended mid-air.

Inturon dashed back into the room carrying a man on his back. The bearcat god guided the man to the ground and jumped up to the trio of Ecrets flying around the ceiling.

A barrage of metal spikes shot out of the water toward Inturon.

He spun around, turning the metal back into water and guided it around his body. The water circled him and turned back toward Ecret.

The water turned to metal, then back to water, obeying the competing commands of each of the gods.

Struggling to stand, the man got on his feet. The specs of light in the air revealed his lemur-painted face. Flashes of spirits surrounded him, holding him upright.

What is he doing here? Why would Inturon bring him into this fight? Another puzzle piece presented itself, but Hagano didn't know where to put it. Even worse, Inturon did.

A popping sound drew Hagano's ear. He turned to the gooey mass he expected Madigan to return from. As if on cue, a hand rose out of the tarry pond. With a simple swipe of the bone sword, Hagano cut it down. Another hand appeared, but fell to the same weapon.

Two Ecrets flew down to Hagano's side. One lifted its wings towards the pool of water and metal that danced above them. The god pulled down a stream of water and drowned the reforming Madigan with it. The tar and water mixed, diluting the acid.

Hagano stepped back to let the Ecrets work. "We have another guest."

"I saw." The two Ecrets spread their wings. "We'll deal with him in a moment."

The mixture of blood and water lifted into the air, forming a liquid sphere. The swirling orb pulled the tar in two directions, separating Ecret's blood from Madigan's acidic power.

The extracted blood slithered through the air, meeting one of the duplicate god's bodies and seeped inside. Color returned to his face and feathers. Whatever this meant, Hagano assumed this was a step closer to Ecret's actual restoration.

The rest of the tar splashed on the ground. It collected into a skeleton, no longer showing any sign of life.

Inturon dropped from the air, landing next to the lemur-faced man. Dodging a shower of blades, Inturon spun around. Rubble collected itself, forming a giant spike. It flew at the two Ecrets that stood between Inturon and Hagano.

The spike burst through one Ecret, then cut through the other before continuing its path to Hagano. It punched through his ribs, removing a large portion of his side and the entirety of an arm. Hagano screamed as he fell onto his back.

The whole world blurred. *Regenerate—no!* He held back his powers. If he let himself die, then it would mean that Inturon killed him. The god would lose his immortality and Ecret could win the fight.

I don't want to die. But he needed to. This could be their only chance—Inturon's fatal mistake. Everything rested on this one decision. Die? Live? The choice was impossible—Ecret or himself.

Darkness crept in on the edge of his vision. He had seconds before the choice was made for him.

A flurry of thoughts flew through him. If Ecret lost his immortality because he killed someone, perhaps Hagano was on the wrong side. The Sylph King wasn't real. No one's soul was doomed to eternal torture, but neither was it guaranteed a peaceful paradise. Did Ecret lie? Did Inturon? Was the weight of the world on Hagano's shoulders? Would dying save his family? *Alessi.* It wouldn't save his brother. His parents had lost one son already. Could Hagano let them lose a second?

The world shrank as the darkness blurred everything around him.

He had to save himself—for his family, for his brother. Alessi wouldn't have wanted him to die.

Heal. The command felt weak. *Heal!*

New muscles grew over new bones. A fresh supply of blood entered his veins. New layers of skin finished the reconstruction. His vision returned, but his heart ached. He chose himself over his god.

Hagano sat up and looked at Inturon. Between them, exactly where an Ecret had just stood—the one struck by the spike—lay a woman.

Hagano scrunched his face and blinked to clear his eyes. He didn't understand what he was seeing. *Jaga?*

She didn't move. She wasn't breathing.

Hagano scrambled to her side. "Jaga!" he yelled into her face. "Jaga!" A large gash in her side left her bleeding. Her leg bent at an unnatural angle. She was dying. *How is she here?! Why is she—?* Click. A terrible realization hit him. He looked to the nearest Ecret with anger burning in his eyes.

This was the god's plan, to disguise Jaga as one of the decoy Ecrets —just like Inturon disguised himself as The Sylph King. Inturon had no reservations about killing fake bodies. He had done so many times already. The bearcat god would kill Jaga eventually. And it had to be Jaga. Ecret needed her because she had a power. That power would make it look like she was one of the duplicates.

"Save her!" Inturon screamed.

"No!" Ecret yelled back. *Trust me, Hagano. Let her go.* Ecret rushed to Hagano's side.

Inturon tackled Ecret. They rolled away.

Hagano took Jaga's hand and bit skin off a finger. He swallowed. Never before had he tried to heal someone else with his power, nor even thought to before now, but he needed to try. Touching Jaga's arm, he summoned the part of his power that could heal her injuries. Instead, a full-grown Jaga appeared. It landed at her feet. Hagano averted his eyes, knowing she wouldn't be clothed.

He tried again, touching Jaga's wounds directly. Nothing.

Jaga didn't wince. She didn't heal. She didn't breathe. Jaga was dead.

Hagano let out a pained cry. "You killed her!" he screamed at both gods. Inturon had thrown the spike that tore through Jaga's body, but Ecret was the one who put a target on her back. *First Alessi. Now Jaga?*

The avian god stopped fighting, letting Inturon land a killing blow. The duplicate body vanished—as did the rest of the Ecrets scattered about the room.

A screeched pierced Hagano's ears, feeling like lightning in his head. He covered them with his hands.

The gem floating in front of Inturon's brow burned brighter than the noon sun, nearly drowning the room in light. A pained scream swelled up, nearly matching the magnitude of the screech.

The light flickered out. The screeching stopped.

Inturon fought to catch his breath. He'd killed someone. He was mortal. His claim was true—killing someone eliminated a god's immortality.

The same thing must have happened to Ecret. The evidence in front of him couldn't be argued. Ecret was a murderer.

Struggling to stand, Inturon made himself a chair and sat in it.

A cough echoed around the room.

Hagano looked to see where it came from, only to find the duplicate body of Jaga laboring to breathe. She was alive and now in the body Hagano had made. "Jaga?"

"Make Ecret a body." She wheezed.

Another Ecret shot into existence. It fluttered a wing, sending a wisp of dust toward Jaga that encircled her before transforming into clothes fit for battle. Ecret looked down to Hagano. "Thank you for putting your trust in me."

A pang of guilt hit him like an arrow. Not only did he choose to save himself—and Jaga—over his god, but he also did not hold faith in the most critical moment. Knowing his betrayal, Hagano couldn't raise his eyes to meet Ecret's. He fought for days to serve him, only to throw it away in a fleeting moment.

The god blood on the floor flowed to Ecret and entered his new body. Once again, it filled him with color and life. Ecret spread out his wings.

Hagano shook his head. "I don't understand." His eyes met Jaga. "How did you come back?"

"I've made the temple a place to catch souls who die. They won't move on so long as they stay inside it." Ecret bowed his head. "That's how I've stayed anchored to this world. But now we have a problem." He gestured to the lemur-faced man as he hobbled to Inturon's side.

"That man?" Hagano pointed.

"Yes." Ecret crouched as if he would spring into the air any second. "He possesses a power similar to the one I used to hold spirits in the temple. He might be able to undo my work and claim my spirit if it leaves my current body."

"No more resurrections." Hagano frowned. "How do we stop him?"

Ecret paused. "Kill him or keep him from activating his power."

"How does he--?" The words barely left Hagano's lips before Ecret cut him off.

"By writing a dead man's name on his skin using their blood. Then that spirit will belong to him." Ecret's tone sobered.

Click. Hagano's eyes widened. "Does he have Alessi? They fought earlier." The lemur-faced man could have taken Alessi's soul or... it was still inside the temple walls.

"I don't know." Ecret bowed.

A team of monkeys ran toward Alessi's body. If his brother could be brought back, he needed a piece of flesh. With any luck, it would work. What were the odds the lemur-faced man could have known Alessi's name when he died and stolen him?

"Alessi, was it?" Inturon's voice sounded labored. He lifted a paw and flicked his wrist.

Alessi's body flew over to Inturon.

Hagano's stomach knotted. "No!"

The lemur-faced man swiped blood off Alessi's corpse and scribbled on his skin. Flashes of light illuminated the writing, spelling Alessi's name on the man's arm.

Changing course, the monkeys spread out to flank the enemy. The command to retrieve a piece of Alessi still guided them.

"Nuisance." Inturon lifted two fists into the air and punched the ground. The floor rumbled like an earthquake.

The stone floor shifted and broke. Pieces of the ceiling crashed all around. A wall collapsed at Hagano's side. Alessi's body was still out of reach. The temple was falling.

The hanging throne fractured into pieces. Rumbling earth tore down wall after wall and ripped holes in the ceiling. Beams of moonlight shot into the room.

Hagano's pulse thumped in his ears. *What do we do? Alessi can't be gone.*

The rumbling stopped. What was once the throne room was nothing more than piles of rocks. But was he too late?

Inturon cracked his neck. "Hagano, command Ecret to kill himself and you can have your brother back."

Hagano froze. He couldn't. He wouldn't... but he wanted to.

"Hagano?" Ecret sounded worried.

Jaga put her hand on Hagano's shoulders. "He wouldn't want you to."

The temptation took root—Hagano could have his brother back. The thought scared him. Was he willing to give up everything for Alessi? Hagano had already chosen himself over Ecret. Did he value Alessi more than himself? Click. He couldn't take the offer. The split second of knowing he could see his brother again erased all his pain, but it wasn't real. Inturon's offer meant nothing. Alessi would never forgive him.

A spark ignited in Hagano's chest, warming him. This warmth felt different than the comforting words of a god—something he'd felt with both Ecret and Inturon. This warmth was peace. Jaga was right —Alessi would not want Hagano to take Inturon's offer. Knowing this, knowing his brother, gave Hagano permission to make the hardest choice of his life. He looked to Inturon and shook his head. "No."

Ecret straightened his posture. "You two get out of here. Leave it to me to kill my brother and his servant."

"Wait." Hagano fought back tears. He couldn't let the lemur-faced man die. Alessi was in his possession. Using that man's power was the only way to get back Alessi. Inturon had torn down the temple walls, taking the spiritual net with them. "Let me fight."

Ecret looked over his shoulder. "This is my fight, Hagano. You're no match for Inturon."

"I can regenerate." Hagano pointed at his chest. "Let me fight him. You can support me without putting yourself in too much danger."

"I can't fight him *and* protect you." Ecret's wings flittered.

"Jaga should leave. She doesn't have powers, but I do." Hagano stepped forward.

"I said no." Ecret's tone deepened.

Something inside Hagano told him he needed to be in this fight. The puzzle pieces sat in front of him, but only a few had arranged themselves in order. But his gut knew something—if Hagano removed himself from the big picture, no arrangement of the pieces led to victory—or Alessi's return. This was his faith—his new faith—a feeling he couldn't explain, but one that he believed in. "I'm not asking for permission."

"Don't make me remove you—"

"No." Hagano balled his hands into fists. "Don't make *me* remove *you.*" He narrowed his eyes. "Sit."

Ecret's legs buckled, forcing him into a sitting position. His body had no choice but to obey Hagano's commands.

A breathy laugh put a smile on Inturon's face. He shook his head. "Pitiful, brother. How far you have fallen to obey the commands of a child."

Hagano released Ecret from his control. "We can do this together."

Ecret glared, but conceded with a nod. "He's mortal now. He won't hesitate to kill you."

"He's weaker too." Hagano tilted his head. "Jaga, time for you to go." He didn't want to argue. *Leave, now.* The command forced Jaga to flee.

Ecret stepped up next to Hagano. "You have a plan?"

Click. Click. Click. The events of the past two days snapped together, forming a path to Inturon's defeat. Hagano couldn't tell if everything had been preordained by a higher power that was now showing its hand or if his mind was cobbling together something that —if he squinted—looked like divine intervention. Hagano and Jaga defeated Lowell's switching power by using it against him. Click. Hagano defeated Eachan with a lie. Click. He used the bone swords to tear down Madigan—weapons so strong that even a god's power couldn't break them. Click. These were his pieces. This was his path.

"I do." Hagano played with his jaw. "I fought a man who had the power to freeze things in time. He's currently frozen in the streets." He took a long breath and focused his thoughts into a command. *Ecret, pretend to go kill Eachan, but instead, fly out of sight and be ready to launch the bone swords from opposite directions.* "Go kill him." The spoken words meant nothing—his power didn't work if he didn't put meaning behind them, which is what he needed to do—remove the meaning, but let Inturon think that killing Eachan was his true command. He wanted Inturon distracted by the idea of Eachan's power when in reality, Ecret would be flying overheard awaiting Hagano's orders.

Ecret flew off. For the plan to work, Hagano had to limit Inturon's switching power to as few targets as possible.

"Bold of you to send away your god." Inturon dropped into a stone seat that formed underneath him.

The lemur-faced man kneeled at Inturon's side.

Hagano walked up to the makeshift throne, stopping a few feet away. "Why did you pretend to be The Sylph King?"

Inturon smirked. "Can you still not see?" He eyed Hagano up and down. "I did it for the same reason Ecret did six hundred years ago—so that I could pretend to kill him and win the hearts of your people."

The response stung. Inturon's actions showed nothing but malice, but Ecret had done the same thing. "Then you've lost already. Ecret is flying through the city as we speak. People will have seen him. Their devotion will be renewed."

"A minor setback." Inturon's cat-like ears flicked. "One easily overcome in a matter of generations." His expression hardened. "Now what are you playing at, killing Eachan and giving me back that power?"

"Are you afraid?" Hagano crossed his arms. He assumed Inturon would have attacked by now, but something held him off.

"Curious," Inturon corrected.

"Now you are the one who doesn't see." Hagano took a step closer.

The god flinched. His upper lip lifted, flashing sharp teeth. He shot out of his chair and took Hagano by the throat.

Hanging in the air, the weight of his body pushed his jaw onto Inturon's paw. The pressure made his teeth feel like they would shatter. He pushed his eyes shut.

Now!

A bone sword flew through the air, straight at Inturon. Buzz. The two switched places. Hagano held Inturon's throat. The sword cut through Hagano, ripping a hole in his chest.

Another sword flew from the opposite direction, cutting through Inturon's stomach. One bone sword stabbed Hagano as the other stabbed Inturon, just as Jaga had done with Lowell. Inturon could have switched places, had his eyes been open. But Hagano had closed his eyes before the switch, leaving Inturon blind after the swap. The god could have frozen the sword the moment it touched him—but that power wasn't with him. Hagano wanted Inturon to try to use it in the moment he needed it. He'd only a fraction of a second to make the attempt. There was no time for anything else, leading to a certain and fatal result. Whatever went through Inturon's mind didn't matter. Hagano's plan worked. The bone swords cut through human and god alike, just as they had done with Madigan's tar.

Inturon screamed. Hagano collapsed, his body repairing itself.

Ecret swooped down from above, landing atop his brother.

Blood spilled out from Inturon's wound and dripped from his mouth. He swiped his nail across the tip of a finger, cutting it off.

"No!" Ecret pinned Inturon's arms, keeping the god from eating the fingertip and regenerating.

A bear appeared at Inturon's head and pushed down on his face, smothering his eyes so the god couldn't switch places. More bears tackled the lemur-faced man as he rose to save his god.

"I'm sorry, brother." Ecret placed the sharp nail of his talon against Inturon's throat.

"Wait!" Hagano yelled.

Ecret froze. His talon trembled, fighting Hagano's command as it tried to cut into Inturon.

Hagano reached out to Ecret. "Don't kill him."

CHAPTER TWENTY-FOUR

THE BROKEN PANTHEON

"Release me, Hagano. Let me end this." Ecret's voice felt fiery and sharp. His talon shook as the dagger-like nail tried to cut into Inturon's throat.

"This is wrong." Hagano shook his head. "He's your brother."

"He wants me dead and you enslaved. What choice do we have?" Ecret's body shook as it fought Hagano's command

"There's another way." Hagano stilled. The bears holding the lemur-faced man freed him. "What's your name?"

The man narrowed his eyes and scanned the scene in front of him. "Urso."

"Urso." Hagano looked into the man's eyes. "I will give you Inturon if you give me back my brother."

The man flinched. His lips moved as if to talk, but he said nothing.

"It's too dangerous, Hagano." Ecret huffed.

Inturon's writhing weakened.

Hagano met the man's gaze. "Your god doesn't have much time before his soul departs. Can you give me back Alessi?"

"Yes." Urso cleared his throat.

Monkeys spread around them, digging for Alessi's corpse. One slipped under a piece of rubble, then climbed up Hagano's leg and placed a piece of flesh in his hand. He swallowed it.

A perfect copy of Alessi's body snapped into being at Hagano's feet.

"Do it." Hagano let out a long breath. He wasn't sure if Urso could be trusted, but he saw no other way to bring Alessi back.

Crouching next to the lifeless Alessi, Urso licked his thumb and crossed out Alessi's name on his arm. He took his thumb to Alessi's forehead and swiped, leaving a faint trail of blood. Urso looked up to Hagano. "Once I free his spirit from my control, he can enter this new body. Let me write Inturon's name on me and I will give Alessi the command."

Hagano nodded back.

Urso approached his god, swept a finger over his wound, and wrote Inturon's name across his arm.

"Good." Hagano bowed his head. *Now kill him.* Ecret's nail sliced Inturon's throat. Blood gushed from the wound.

Flashes of light lit up Inturon's name on Urso's arm.

Hagano crouched next to Inturon's bleeding hand and picked up the tip of Inturon's finger that he'd cut off. He paused—avoiding Ecret's eyes.

"This isn't a good idea." Ecret stepped next to him.

Hagano's mind blanked. He had no response. He didn't know if he was making the most dangerous choice imaginable. But it felt right—and not just because he would get Alessi back. When he'd eaten a piece of Ecret, waves of animals burst out of him and his chest caught fire. Pain—he'd suffered so much of it over the last two days. No—it had been months. Ever since that horse kicked his shoulder, he'd spent every day trying to avoid it. Every movement, every choice, every day begged the same question—will it hurt? Yet here he was, about to throw a piece of a god's finger down his throat, knowing it would feel like agony. And for what? His enemy?

No. It was for Ecret. It was for Inturon. It was for their relationship as brothers. Hagano had lost his only brother twice—once when Hagano's injury drove a wedge between them and a second time when Alessi had died. No amount of pain or anger or hurt could change the fact that brothers should take care of each other.

He threw the bit of flesh in his mouth and swallowed.

An eerie silence permeated the air. There was no explosion of animals. No fire. No chaos. No pain.

He turned to Urso. "Free Alessi's spirit and I will make a body for Inturon."

Closing his eyes, Urso exhaled through his nose.

Alessi gasped for breath.

"Alessi!" Hagano crouched and gripped his brother's shoulders. "Are you okay?"

Panting, Alessi looked back and forth like a child waking from a nightmare. "Am I alive?"

"Yes." A stream of tears rolled down Hagano's cheeks.

A cloud of dust kicked up over Alessi's body and clung to his skin, forming clothes. Hagano helped him to his feet. He looked to the dead Inturon, then over to Urso. "As promised."

A duplicate body of the bearcat god snapped into being. Urso again crossed out the name, swiped the brow, closed his eyes, and let out a breath.

Inturon's eyes shot open. He jumped to his feet.

"Sit still." Hagano held out his hand. "Don't attack us and don't say a word."

The new Inturon sat down cross-legged, following Hagano's command. The god's eyes peered at Hagano with a burning fury.

A sullen look washed over Urso's face.

One last puzzle piece needed to fall in place for Hagano's plan to work. "If your name is Inturon, stand up."

Inturon stood.

Hagano nodded. "If your name is Mr. Fuzzy-face, sit down."

Inturon remained standing.

"Good." Hagano clasped his hands together.

Ecret paced. "What are you doing, Hagano?"

"Testing something." He cleared his throat. "I needed to make sure this body—" He motioned to Inturon. "Would obey an if-then command. Simple commands make sense, like touch your toes or jump up and down. I assumed they would understand an if-then command, since my chickens did when I used them as an alarm system, but now I know for sure."

"This is your plan to control him?" Ecret straightened his back, making him all that much taller.

Folding his arms, Hagano rocked on his heels. "Yes. This is my plan to control... both of you."

The two gods snapped their gaze to Hagano.

Ecret shook his head. "Hagano, no."

Hagano shushed him. *Don't talk.* He took in a deep breath. "Neither of you will hurt the other. Inturon will go back to his country." He stepped up to Inturon, looking him square in the eyes. "You will never set foot in Ecret's land again. You will never tell, command, or ask someone to harm Ecret or anyone belonging to this country again." The words made Inturon clench his jaw. "If you do, you will kill those who you've ordered to do harm, then take your own life immediately."

Turning to Ecret, Hagano relaxed his shoulders—suddenly aware how tense they'd become. "Ecret, you also will never send someone to do harm to Inturon or his followers. You, yourself, will never harm Inturon again. You may enter Inturon's territory, but only if your intentions are purely peaceful. If you violate any of these commands, you will kill those who you've ordered to do harm and then yourself immediately."

Ecret bowed his head.

"Am I missing something or will these commands suffice?"

Ecret looked to Hagano, but didn't say a word.

"You can both talk now."

"This is new territory for us gods, Hagano." Ecret paused. "But yes. That sounds sufficient."

Inturon gave a quick nod and turned to Ecret. "They'll come for us, you know. Now that we're weak."

Ecret kept silent.

"One more thing." Hagano approached Inturon, but turned to

look at Ecret. "When I was dying in the streets, I had a vision. You told me you could not give me a second power. It would kill me. Is that right?"

Ecret nodded. "Yes."

Hagano licked his lips. "But can I be given the same power twice?"

"What do you mean?" Ecret cocked his head to the side. "I can't give you a power I don't currently possess."

"He wants *my* power." Inturon crossed his arms. "Clever, I admit, to keep me from trying to steal a piece of my original body and make one I control."

The orange glow around Ecret's eyes shimmered. "It would be harmless, in theory."

Taking a breath, Hagano closed his eyes and focused on what his heart was telling him. He needed to take the risk. "Give me your power to create animals from the flesh I have eaten."

Inturon gripped Hagano's mouth. A burst of energy shot from his palm, across Hagano's tongue, and down his throat. A heat burnt his tongue, then faded. Inturon retracted his paw.

"Now go." Hagano waved toward the temple plaza.

Inturon put Urso on his back, sprinted over the temple rubble and disappeared out of sight.

A wave of relief washed over Hagano, sending him to his knees. Everything felt lighter as if a puppeteer were pulling up on his strings. The enemy was gone, his minions defeated. Hagano's muscles relaxed, but felt like sinking rocks drifting to the bottom of a pond. An exhaustion found his body, but not his mind. Everything felt clear. "Is it over?"

Ecret looked around. "For now."

Click. Something nagged at Hagano, a suppressed thought that now rose to the surface. "Lord..." The word tasted strange, like it no longer applied. "...what was the endling Inturon was searching for?"

Ecret bowed his head and shifted in place. He nodded slightly, hinting at a difficult inner dialogue. "Follow me." The god walked towards the bowels of the temple, winding through the rubble with nearly every step.

Hagano hustled to catch up.

Ecret escorted Hagano through the temple. Minutes passed before he finally spoke. "Hagano—" The god's voice faltered. "The memory you possess, of me and Inturon, is thousands of years old— long before the world spiraled into chaos and bloodshed. The gods have been at war with each other far longer than we were ever at peace." Ecret tilted his head. "Inturon, it seems, decided to end the fight once and for all."

"Did you know he would come to kill you?"

The god hummed for a moment. "I hoped he wouldn't, but I anticipated that he would. Inturon's spies discovered my mortality. How exactly, I'm not sure. But I sent the Hallux to guard my secret. He failed. When he died, I knew they would come, but I did not know when."

Hagano followed Ecret around a corner. "But what changed? How did you and Inturon go from such a happy, loving relationship to something so... hateful?"

The god looked up, but kept up his pace. "Anger is always born of another emotion. In Inturon's case, I believe his animosity comes from his loneliness."

"Loneliness?" Hagano bit his lip. "Doesn't he have millions of people living under his command?"

"Inturon never cared for humans. And his loneliness..." Ecret ducked into an adjacent hall. "...is my fault. We were allies for a very long time."

"What happened?"

"I *did* care for humans." Ecret lifted a wing, spreading beads of light down the dark hallway in front of them. "What you saw, when we were young, is from a time early in our brotherhood. We gods inherited this world from our father when we were small. And then we grew. We gained powers. We cultivated civilizations and sent them to war, all for the sake of having more power than our siblings." Ecret stopped, but kept his gaze focused in front of him. "It was a game to us."

Hagano stopped, keeping at Ecret's side. "Are all your siblings so... hostile?"

"Yes, in their own ways." A moment of quiet passed. Ecret started walking again.

Hagano stepped quickly to keep up. "What changed?" This story sounded nothing like the Ecret he knew, but if he learned anything today it was that he didn't truly know Ecret.

"I did." The god took a deep breath. "I changed. The wars were endless. My people were always suffering. What we were doing, what I was doing, was meant to bring me glory. But I began to question myself. I started wondering, do humans exist to glorify the gods or do the gods exist to glorify humans?"

The thought put up a wall in Hagano's head. "I don't understand. Glorify humans?"

The two of them started down a stairwell.

"Yes. To make you better than you are. To teach you peace, sympathy, kindness. I believe my purpose is to elevate mankind. Exalt you, to the best of my abilities. Which is..." Ecret turned a corner. "... admittedly, lacking."

They reached the bottom of the stairs, made a sharp right, and entered a dark hallway. More drops of light spread.

Ecret stopped in the middle of the hall and turned to a seemingly random point in the wall. He tapped a talon against a brick, which dislodged. A cloud of dust puffed out of the stone bricks, revealing a hidden door. "Do you still have that key I gave you?"

The key! Hagano smacked his hand against his pant pocket. "I can't believe I almost forgot about it." He withdrew the key and pushed it into the lock of the door. He paused and looked up into Ecret's glowing eyes. "I never found out what was in the book you wanted me to find."

The god nodded. "Instructions and a map... to here."

"Where are we?" The bowels of the temple always seemed endless to Hagano. For all he knew, they'd walked to the other side of the world.

"Turn your wrist and find out."

A metallic click sounded as he turned the key. The door creaked open. Another long hallway greeted them.

Ecret stepped inside. "We're almost there."

The two kept walking.

Ecret scattered more light. "It may be of no consolation, but I am truly sorry." He slowed down. "I regret the lies about The Sylph King and the promise of eternal paradise."

"Why did you lie?" A thousand questions whirled in Hagano's head.

"I've lived for millenia. I watched people murder, steal, deceive, and dishonor each other in every imaginable way. And I wanted to glorify them, but I didn't know how. So I decided to tell people about an eternal reward for a pious life. Some changed. Some didn't. I expounded on that lie. For those who needed fear to change, I invented The Sylph King. Even more corrected their behavior, but it took many generations before a virtual peace took effect. Once a general righteousness took hold, I merely maintained it."

"I still don't understand something. How did you lose your immortality? Who did you... kill?" Hagano followed Ecret down another winding staircase.

"There is a universal balance. As immortals, gods cannot interrupt that balance. We cannot lose our lives, so we cannot take a life. That isn't to say it is impossible. We can kill, but the cost of causing death is losing our invulnerability to death." Ecret stopped in the middle of a hallway and opened up another door that Hagano hadn't noticed. "However, my immortality wasn't lost because I took a life. I discovered another way to interrupt that balance."

Deep inside the recesses of the temple, the two stopped in front of a statue of Ecret. The god tapped it with a toe. The wall behind it opened up into a hidden room filled with light and all manner of plant life. The two stepped inside.

A pond of luminous green water sat in the middle of the room. Vines sprouted from it and wove up and down a trellis. Floating in the middle of the pond lay a small creature made of white feathers with black tips, a long neck, a human face, and five black horns barely poking out of its head.

Hagano shot Ecret a confused look, then stared at the pond. The creature inside it looked exactly like a young Ecret—the same face he saw in the water inside Ecret's memory.

"This is the endling—the *new* endling." Ecret tapped the water with the tip of his wing. Ripples spread.

"I didn't know there could be more gods." Hagano sat next to the pool. "Is he sleeping?"

"No. He's incubating."

That two sat down and watched the young Ecret as if he would spring to life at any moment.

"Wait." Hagano pointed at Ecret. "Did you lay an egg?"

"No." Ecret responded defensively. "I'm male."

Hagano shrugged. "Well, I don't know how it works."

"The godling is my offspring—one I made with the very power that you now possess."

"Really? My power?" Hagano examined his hands as if looking at them for the first time.

"Yes." Ecret began to circle the pond. "I was trying to understand why the human duplicates I created were lifeless."

"Oh. The same thing happens when *I* try." He thought back to creating a copy of himself and how odd it was seeing himself naked.

Ecret nodded. "I know."

"Did you figure it out?"

Stretching out his wings, Ecret took a long breath. "No. Every animal I found would come to life, but not people. The only thing I hadn't tried was god-flesh. And when I tried that..." Ecret stepped into the pool and craned his neck to look down at his child. "This happened. The young god was born—alive, but undeveloped. I built this place for it to gestate."

"How long has it been down here?"

"About forty years."

Hagano didn't know what to say and Ecret kept his focus on the pond.

The stillness brought Hagano's mind back up into the throne room where Inturon's body laid. "Inturon. You'll have to hide his corpse."

Ecret stepped out of the pond and tapped the floor. "You're quite right." The god stretched out his wings and lifted his head. A hole opened up in the room and Inturon's corpse dropped through it. "There. This is the safest room in the temple." Stones gathered from every direction and assembled themselves into a coffin around the dead god.

"I have one more question for you." Hagano bowed his head.

"And I have one for you."

"Yes?" asked Hagano, suddenly nervous about what his god might say.

"Why did you choose to save Inturon? Was it all for your brother?" Ecret's voice returned to its usual melodic rhythm.

Hagano thought for a moment. There was a sense of gratitude inside him. Inturon showed him truth and gave back Hagano's arms. The feeling was small and hardly compared to the atrocities committed by Inturon. But it was there. *No, it wasn't that.* Hagano sighed. "Brothers should never kill each other. You'd have to live forever knowing you took the life of someone you loved. And Inturon's people... they shouldn't have to know how it feels to lose the one they worship. I know that pain. If Inturon died, everyone would suffer." Hagano swallowed what felt like a lump in his throat. "I guess I hoped that somehow your relationship would mend in time."

Ecret looked down.

"What will happen to you and Inturon when I die? Will your bodies vanish?" It seemed like a thought Hagano should have had before he saved Inturon.

"No, our bodies will remain. We will live on for however long our mortality lasts." Ecret's words filled the air with his typical warmth. "But your commands will lose their power."

Hanging his head, Hagano played with his feet. "Sorry. I guess you have about sixty years to make amends."

"Was that your question?" Ecret looked over the pond. "If my body would vanish with your death?"

"Oh. No." Hagano's face flushed red.

"Then what would you like to ask me?"

Hagano sat quiet, collecting his thoughts before he could put them into words. He was an eighteen-year-old kid who had no real position or authority. But now he had a power, a godly power, and with that power he controlled two gods. The gods were always above him. Had he brought them low? Or had he made himself high? Hagano looked up at his Ecret. "What am I?"

Silence.

The god stood still, expressionless.

Fumbling over his words, Hagano kept talking. "I have power over two gods, but I'm just a person."

"Yes, you are a person." Ecret nodded. "Honestly, I don't know what you are—something new."

Hagano sat and thought for a moment. He assumed Ecret did the same because neither of them said anything. But he was something new. *Is that a good thing?* He didn't have answers and it seemed like no one did.

"Let's get back. I'm sure there are people worried about the both of us." Ecret stood and the two of them travelled back through the winding halls, the hidden passageways, and the many staircases that filled the depths of the earth.

Once they reached the throne room, Hagano could see that Jaga and Alessi had collected the bodies of the fallen guards and placed them side by side.

Many of the dead were unrecognizable—warped by Madigan's tar or crushed by the debris when Inturon destroyed the throne room.

Jaga bowed her head. Clasping her hands together, she whispered, "May their spirits find rest in paradise."

The four of them took a moment of silence.

The words Jaga spoke sent a chill down Hagano's spine. The guards would not be resting in paradise. Where their spirits actually were, he didn't know, but paradise was fiction.

Hagano looked at his brother and smiled. He was alive—they both were. "Alessi, will you go home and let mom and dad know we are safe. I don't want them worrying a moment longer."

"I'll come too." Jaga stood up straight. "I'd like to thank them for their help."

Alessi crossed his arms and shot a look to his brother. "Aren't you coming?"

"I will be. But first..." Hagano turned to Ecret. "I need your help with something."

Hagano led Ecret out of the temple and back to the street where he left Eachan frozen to his own power. The Inturoni was still there, a python in his mouth, another around his throat, and a third nearly biting his eye. Hagano walked up to Eachan and discarded each snake.

Eachan unfroze.

Gagging and coughing, Eachan fought for air. He gripped the bite mark on his arm. "Are you gonna kill me?"

"No," Hagano said. "Lowell and Madigan are dead. Inturon is now under my control and heading back to his own country. Your allies have paid for what they did. And you have nothing more than a snake bite. Pythons aren't venomous, by the way."

Eachan frowned, looking embarrassed.

"So no, we will not kill you. We will enlist you. Once you have paid for your crimes, then you may return home. If that's alright with Ecret."

Ecret placed a talon on Eachan's head. "Do you accept your servitude?"

Eachan stared down Hagano. "I suppose I have no choice."

Removing his talon, Ecret revealed a sigil on Eachan's forehead. It burned into his skin, smoking and sizzling. A drop of blood rolled down his face.

"Great." Eachan scowled.

"I think it's time for you to go home, Hagano." Ecret leaned down to whisper in Hagano's ear. "But be careful who you tell your tale. Information can be dangerous." He pulled away, then leaned back in.

"I also want your help. Too much blood has been shed in my name, but I will continue to try and glorify my people."

Hagano smiled. "I'm sorry too, by the way."

Ecret gave him a puzzled look.

"I..." Hesitation choked Hagano. "I healed myself. I knew if I died, Inturon would have become mortal. I chose myself over... everyone."

"I forgive you," the god replied.

The words put tears in Hagano's eyes, blurring his vision.

"It was one choice. Compare that to every choice you made over the past two days. You chose to fight for me, for yourself, your family, and your people. You went up against the enemy over and over, despite little hope. You made dozens, if not hundreds, of choices that put everyone else above yourself. A moment of weakness doesn't erase all others, nor does it outweigh it." The god placed a wing on Hagano's shoulder. "The world isn't as black and white as we would like it to be. You are not perfect. Nor am I." Ecret looked up to the sky.

The dawn broke over the mountains, turning the landscape a pleasant shade of orange.

"I am sorry I am not the god you want me to be."

"Maybe not," Hagano admitted. "But you are mine."

Ecret smiled and bowed his head. "Thank you."

Hagano smiled back, then left for home. The last time he saw his family, he had no arms, little hope, and a wounded Jaga over his shoulder. He could only imagine how much his parents had worried.

His mind couldn't help but revisit the fight with Inturon and his choice to force a peace. It didn't feel real. He was no one. Just a courier. But now he had power over gods. *What am I? Something new. Some... thing?* A newfound sympathy for Ecret emerged. Power was not easy to wield.

The moment his house came into view, Hagano saw his mother embracing Alessi and crying into his chest. Jaga stood at the doorway, talking to his father. Alessi pointed at Hagano. Their mother turned to look down the street. She ran to greet her son. Hagano too ran at full speed.

With joyful tears in both their eyes, Hagano wrapped his mother in a warm embrace. Joining their family at the doorstep, Hagano hugged his father, then turned to Alessi. They stared at each other.

The whole world settled into a unifying calm. Birds chirped in the distance. Morning sunlight warmed Hagano's face. He grinned at Alessi as the tension in his muscles evaporated. Alessi was alive. Ecret was alive. Hagano had been healed.

Alessi put his hands on Hagano's shoulders and squeezed them. His face flushed. He cleared his throat. Water entered the corners of his eyes. "Thank you."

Hagano stepped forward and embraced his brother. "I love you too."

～

END OF BOOK ONE

ALSO BY ADAM BERG

Rainbringer — Available now on Amazon

16-year-old Yara is locked inside a bamboo hut, sentenced to starve to death in order to save her island. As she weakens, a storm protects the island inhabitants from ravenous monsters emerging from the deep.

As the days without food take their toll, the truth surfaces—the tradition was built on lies. Yara journals her investigation into the Rainbringer history —until an unseen hand starts writing back.

ABOUT THE AUTHOR

Adam Berg is a real human boy and not a figment of his dog's imagination. He started his career in sketch comedy, spent six years writing and acting in Studio C, and now works for JK! Studios. Feed him cookies, please.

Find him online—
  Instagram: heyadamberg
  Twitter: theadamberg

www.ingramcontent.com/pod-product-compliance
Lightning Source LLC
Chambersburg PA
CBHW071305210626
46818CB00015B/3029